THE BROKEN CITY

MARY E. TWOMEY

MARY E. TWOMEY, LLC

THE BROKEN CITY

Book Two in the Last Deadblood Series

By

Mary E. Twomey

For Rachel Schurig.

Thank you for listening to me whine and pretending I wasn't being super way annoying.

ABOUT THE BROKEN CITY

Colette Kennedy is ready to destroy anyone in her path when the city turns its back on the people she loves.

When Colette decides the West End has been ignored long enough, she will stop at nothing to set things right. Though there are many who oppose vampires being treated as equals, Colette knows it is time to use her mother's legacy to give them a fighting chance.

The forbidden romance is heating up, especially when Rome and Colette find ways to sneak away from the city that threatens to tear them apart. But when their secret relationship is exposed, Colette isn't sure if her family will turn on her, or if she can have what she's always dreamed of—a peaceful life with the man she loves.

THE VAMPIRE AND THE DEADBLOOD
COLETTE

It's hard to keep my nerves at bay when Rome and my father have their scheduled meetings.

Though our relationship is new and predictably rocky, we have struck a deal. Rome agreed not to bring up my embarrassing "I love you" slip I made a few days ago on the phone while I was at the movie theater, and I agreed not to mention him almost breaking up with me because things are most certainly going to be complicated going forward.

It's going as well as one might expect the very first vampire-human pairing in history to unfold.

If anyone found out that the head of the Valentino family was calling me—the Last Deadblood—every night, they wouldn't believe it.

Of course, no one would believe Rome has a poetic soul in the first place. They assume just because he inherited the mess of the West End from his father, that he doesn't appreciate the finer things.

But the man makes me raspberry cannoli from scratch. He reads me poetry on the phone at night.

He kisses like a filthy, filthy dream.

We have fallen into our rhythm of clandestine phone calls and precious flirts, as well as a once-a-week Wednesday date. Though I wish we could have a normal relationship, I've always known that was not in the cards for me, no matter which man is at my side. Frankly, I'm surprised I haven't received any threats from the revolution, claiming they will abduct me if I don't give them my blood voluntarily.

Of course they want my blood; it's the one thing that can kill vampires without fail. People fear what they don't understand.

They certainly don't understand Rome, or the entire race of people who were given a raw deal. The vampires are too beaten down to demand better.

Or perhaps the humans have stopped listening.

That's what these meetings between my father and Rome are supposed to be. The sheriff is supposed to listen and be helpful (imagine that), while Rome makes an attempt at trust.

It's a stretch for them both, but it happens twice a month outside my salon, and I love it every time. I want people to walk by my salon and see progress. I want them to see my sign that reads *Vampires and Humans Welcome* and feel a sense of peace about the world.

I really wish other businesses would follow suit. Midtown is a neutral space between the East and West sides of Mayfield. Still, my salon is one of the very few businesses that will actually cater to both races.

One step at a time, even if that step is tiny and feels like it is getting us nowhere.

The salon is busy, which makes me happy. But when the two show up for their biweekly chat, it's like a cloud comes over the lighthearted atmosphere. People inch away from the window but keep their eyes on the two heads of the rival families who used to be close.

Instead of lighting up like a giant Christmas tree at the sight of Rome entering my salon, I let Rachel greet him because she is tending to the front desk for this hour. Rome hands her a sealed envelope and tells her it's for the owner without meeting my eyes. Usually it's an effort to pretend I am uncomfortable with him in my business, but not such an effort today, given that he tried to break up with me the last time I saw him.

Rome is stunning, even from a distance. His obsidian hair highlights the brightness of his ice blue eyes. His angular jaw is strong and casts emotion so well that he rarely has need for a smile. He is tall and leonine, with broad shoulders and a trim waist. I never cared much about the uniform the Valentino men all wear—white dress shirt with the sleeves rolled, black fitted trousers and a silver belt buckle—but on Rome, it is perfection.

Then my father enters a minute later.

Now I'm sweating.

The sheriff doesn't know I am dating a vampire. *He couldn't possibly*, I tell myself. *I'm being perfectly normal.*

My father and I exchange a few words to convince each other that we have absolutely no bad blood between us, which is a constant dance we do. We don't talk about the fact that he sent me away when I was sick. We don't talk about him letting us all down by alienating the West End and doing a bad job at law enforcement for so long. Because of his bigoted negligence, there is precious little hope we will be able to dig Mayfield out of the hole in which it is mired.

No, we don't talk about any of it. I'm a good daughter.

Mostly.

"I'll be out there with the Valentinos. You still okay with us meeting here?" my father asks, his chin lowered as if he actually cares about my response.

His hair is thinner these days, his skin dry and sagging. Even his thick neck is wrinkled. Though he is only in his sixties, he looks far more weathered. I'm not sure if it's the job or if something deeper is going on, but if not for his dismissive attitude toward the things that matter, I might think him an older relative of the man who sent me away when I was only fifteen. That man was scary to argue with. This man—the aged one standing before me—still inspires fear in my soul, but there is a weariness to him that makes me think new ideas might actually have a fighting chance.

I wave my hand to dismiss his words. "It's fine. Don't shoot up the place when you two bulls disagree over which one of you knits the prettiest tea cozy."

The sheriff snorts an airy laugh at my quip before exiting.

Huh. My father hasn't been coming in to greet me before his meetings with Rome. He did once when I cut his hair, but never since. We do a pleasant "you don't exist if I don't look at you" sort of dance, which has served us both well.

My steps are measured as I retrieve the sealed envelope from my mailbox slot and slip into my office. My door locks and I rush to my desk, tearing open the envelope to find...

What am I looking at? Ledger sheets?

A small note from Rome slips out. "I know Martin's Dry Cleaners is involved in the drug game that's killing the West End. Stayed up late trying to find the hole in their books. Stayed up later thinking of you. Maybe you can be my second pair of eyes."

A girlish smile takes over my features as an exhale rocks my body. He's not going to call me out on my embarrassing "I love you" slip, nor is he breaking up with me in a letter.

Thank goodness. We can pretend neither of those things ever happened.

Memories of our most recent dip in the lake flood my mind, bringing my gaze to my wrist.

The white gold diamond bracelet is far too dressy for work, but I can't help myself. He clasped it around my wrist the last time we went to our beach. I was in cutoffs and a sweatshirt, my hood on to fend off the brunt of the chilly autumn weather. We'd been laughing together and making out under our favorite tree when he fixed it on my wrist.

We get one date a week, and we spend it on a stretch of beach no one frequents this time of year. We wanted to be so far away that no one from Mayfield would see us.

When I gaped at the luxury, he held up a hand to stave off my spluttering. "For the record, this is me holding myself back. I put back the necklace I wanted to buy you last week, and I walked away from the bulletproof windows I wanted your car outfitted with two weeks ago."

I'd stared at the bracelet, much like I am doing now, wondering how my life took such a dramatic turn. Rome's affection is lavish and loud, even when we have to be silent about it.

Rome is a constant puzzle. He is committed to us completely, but whenever he realizes the danger to me that might come because of our relationship, he gets this altruistic streak that tells him to break things off for my safety.

I do my best to enjoy our relationship while it's here. While the world will still leave us alone.

Though I have an appointment in ten minutes, I comb over the copy of the ledger from Martin's Dry Cleaners. At first glance, things appear in order, but I know better than to brush off Rome's gut. If he thinks this business has something to do with the dreaded and highly addictive halluci-blend coming into Mayfield, then this is the place to look.

Some of the products they are buying I am not educated on, so I look up every single one, making a note of each business they've bought from so I can investigate their dealings, too.

This is turning into a longer project than I had anticipated. The spreadsheet I am putting together on my laptop is practically groaning at the amount of data that might actually lead to nothing important.

When I am interrupted by a knock, I cringe at the time. I am five minutes late for my client, which is not acceptable.

Victor pops his head in with a smile. "I shampooed your one o'clock. You want me to cut her, too?" He adjusts the brunette bun atop his head.

There's not a drop of judgment or anything passive aggressive in his question. Victor is being a team player, which is a truly good feeling. I love that I have surrounded myself with such solid people.

However, I despise that I am the one for which they are picking up slack. That's not me. "I've got it. Thank you, Victor. Count on taking my tip from this one, okay? Sorry. I got caught up."

Victor high-fives me and then runs a finger over his eyebrows to straighten them. "Don't sweat it. I've got your back, Boss."

To make up for my tardiness, I am extra chatty and on the ball while I tend to my client. When the next one comes in after I finish up with her, I notice that Rome is still at the table with my father.

They are usually done by now.

Orlando stands behind his cousin like a sentry, silent but visible enough to enforce respect. I hate that my father needs the visual reminder to be a decent person.

Orlando looks much like Rome, only taller and with a more intimidating musculature.

Also, I've seen Rome smile, but Orlando doesn't bother with levity, as it doesn't get the job done.

Usually, their meetings don't last more than half an hour, but the two are glaring at each other with an intensity that twists my stomach.

I grumble at the two under my breath, even though I know they cannot hear me. "Nice attempt at peace, guys. I'm sure everyone in Mayfield is convinced."

I don't hold my father in the high esteem many girls do their fathers, but part of me does wish he could take a shine to Rome. I also don't care if my eldest brother, Fintan, gets along with Rome, but it would be nice. Fintan doesn't really like me all that much, so I can't expect him to like my boyfriend.

But if Declan—my favorite brother and closest friend in the world—lives his whole life hating my secret boyfriend, that is going to be hard to swallow. One day, I will have to tell Declan. We don't keep secrets from each other. Not like this one.

My mouth goes dry as a horrible thought occurs to me.

I very much care if Rome is telling my father that we are dating.

He wouldn't do that. It's suicide.

My palms are sweating. My fingers start to twitch, so as soon as I finish the cut I am working on, I quickly excuse myself to my office once more, digging through my purse for my pills.

I swallow one without the need for water to choke it down. I can't take chances today, or I'll have a flareup at work. Stress is a major contributor to setting off the condition I swore to my doctor up and down I had mastered.

I count to sixty, knowing the fast-acting stuff is well on its way to helping me regain control before I lose myself completely.

Cutting hair with trembling hands is a bad idea. My

condition leaves no room for my pride or trying to muscle through.

I place the flat of my hands atop my desk, breathing in and out slowly to make sure no part of me is shaking.

This is *my* business. *My* salon. I don't need to feel anxious here.

When I walk back into the bustle of my business, I notice the two bulldogs outside at the table have traded up from glares to a full-on argument. My father is talking wildly with his hands while Rome is sitting back in his seat, adding a word here and there with a curled upper lip.

The people sitting on my white leather couches in the waiting area aren't reading their magazines or looking at their phones. They are staring out the picture window at the burgeoning feud framed perfectly before them in front of my business.

My stylists are more intent on their work than ever before, only they're all silent, pretending they don't see the storm brewing outside.

This is not the atmosphere I set out to create. I have lavender walls, for crying out loud. That color bespeaks civility, not angry men gunning for each other.

I am wearing a short, teal high-waisted pencil skirt with a fitted baby blue blouse tucked into it. My hair has been woven into two French braids that twist into a chocolate-brown bun at the base of my neck.

I clearly dressed for a fun, peaceful environment.

I did not get out of bed today to referee their fighting.

I am an adult. I don't have to tolerate my father's tantrums anymore. I can stand up to him. I can make my voice matter.

"Be right back," I sing to Rachel and Victor, who stiffen and cast me warning looks to be careful.

Nah. Careful gets you nowhere.

I roll my shoulders back, draw myself up and stalk outside. I pull strength from the click of my heels. The formidable sound lets people know that a reckoning is coming.

"You think I have the resources to deal with your mess?" my father booms.

"Good afternoon, Miss Kennedy," Rome greets me, ignoring my father's temper.

How it's not clear that I am infatuated with this man, I'm not sure.

Rome meets my gaze and I wet my lower lip on instinct.

Not now, dummy.

I pull over a third chair to join the two heads at the table—something not even Orlando has the gall to do. I cross my left leg over my right and drum my fingertips on the lavender-painted table. "Good afternoon, Rome. Sheriff. Seems we have a bit of a problem, here. I've got it in my silly little head that I'm running a business, but you two seem to think that this salon exists solely for you to yell at each other. Care to share with the teacher what it is we're shouting about?"

My father doesn't like my condescending sing-song tone, which is exactly why I'm using it. He combs his fingers through his thinning light brown curls. Then he sniffs and swipes at his bulbous nose. "None of your business."

I force a throaty laugh. "Actually, it's none of *their* business." I point to my customers inside the building. "But this whole place is *my* business. *All* my business. So you're going to tell me what's going on, and you're going to do it with a smile. The peace treaty is only as solid as the smiles on your faces, so sell it better than this." My grin has a maniacal gleam to it as I lock eyes on my father. "Come on, now. Smile for the cameras. Everyone is watching us."

My father flinches because those are the exact words he used to say to me every time we went out in public when I was a little girl.

No, I am not about to make this easy for him.

2

ROME AND THE SHERIFF
COLETTE

Rome takes my scolding with humility and gives me the information I want. "I'm having a bit of trouble with a few dealers in my area. I was hoping to get a little backup from the sheriff. I'm tired of public arrests, though. They do nothing for morale. I'd prefer it done the same way the East End arrests are handled: humanely. And with options of rehab offered before a sentence comes down. You know, like how the East Enders are treated."

I throw my head back, donning a smile so fake, I'm sure I look like a mannequin. "Oh, that's all? Of course the sheriff will take care of that for you. It's his whole job. Why should vampires be criminalized and humans get a slap on the wrist? That's silly."

My father glares at me, holding up a hand to stop my chipper input. "Don't, Coco. This doesn't concern you."

I point to the people in my salon, who are still watching our exchange. "Actually, it concerns everyone in Mayfield. How many arrests are you making in the East End for drug dealing, Sheriff? Because drug use is no different in the two territories."

"I'm protecting my people, alright?"

I lean my elbows on the table, fixing my father with a pointed stare to juxtapose my lighthearted smile. "Funny. I thought you were supposed to protect and serve the whole of Mayfield. Are you not up for the job anymore?" I reach out and place my hand gently atop his. "Listen, if you're overwhelmed, you should take a break. Maybe a long vacation. It's for your own good. Mayfield is a stressful place. Let me handle the city while you go relax."

My sweet offer is a threat wrapped in lace. It's the same speech he gave me before he shipped me overseas so he wouldn't have to deal with the mess my life had become. It was "for my own good" that I was sent away.

"Let me handle the city while you go relax," was how he effectively dismissed me from my life, and from his.

After that, he pulled some very illegal strings and got power of attorney, taking my choices away from me so I had to stay away even longer.

My father stiffens. I can tell he remembers the conversation well. His cheeks turn pink while his lips purse. I expect the defiance in his eyes. I anticipate the cold sneer.

Instead what I get is raw defeat.

Weird.

The sheriff turns his hand over so he can hold onto mine. His grip is unfamiliar, his hands coarse and dry. "Maybe you're right. I do need to look at this from a new angle."

I don't know what to say to that. I was prepared for a fight, not a surrender.

What's his angle?

My father runs his tongue over his top row of teeth, still holding onto my hand, as if that's a thing we do. "I want things to change. I do, Rome." He meets my boyfriend's eyes with meekness this time—an emotion of which I didn't think him capable. "Maybe you're right. Maybe I have to change more than this."

I take my father's humility with confusion. His words are a shock to my system. They burn away my previous snark.

My voice softens because I am unfamiliar with the bully backing down. I was gearing up to gut him with my next point.

Instead, my words come out like honey. "Rome trusts you. He respects you. It's why he came to you for help. Look at him." I wait until my dad complies, staring at Rome in a new light. "See the weight on his shoulders? Daddy Valentino put part of it there, and we added our share by turning our backs on him, criminalizing his people." I meet my father's gaze with a scolding that goes beyond this situation. "We can do better than shut out a person who's in pain."

It's another well-aimed dagger. We don't talk about my time overseas. It's a sore subject I have never known how to broach. Yet here with Rome, out in the open air veiled in kindness, my silent agony finally gets its day in the sun.

I was in pain, and my father sent me away, ignoring me until I learned not to call for him anymore.

My father squeezes my hand. "Today I'm going to reassign my teams. There is going to be equal policing on both ends." Rome perks up as the sheriff runs his free hand over his face. "No. I can do better than that." His grumbling is met with another step forward into a better future. "If a dealer is picked up, they're going to be booked for the same crime, no matter their race."

My mouth falls open. I have no frame of reference for my father listening to me, so we are in new territory.

The sheriff shocks me further as he keeps going. "I'll have a talk with the judge in the county who I deal with most. He'll listen to me. We golf together often enough. We'll come up with a judgment that's the same across the board—vampire or human. If a dealer of halluci-blend is caught, he gets thirty days of rehab and six months behind bars. No exceptions, no variations. Does that sound fair? Now, I can't guarantee it, but what he does, the other judges usually follow suit."

Rome's mouth drops open. "Fair is exactly what that sounds like. That's all I'm asking."

My father leans forward, jabbing his finger to the center of the table. "It's not going to solve everything, though. I need you to understand that."

"Understood. Thank you." Rome sits up and leans forward, tucking away his wounded ego. "I am not my father, Elias. I know we played our part in ruining our end of the city. I'm breaking my back trying to fix it as best I can."

My father lowers his chin. "I know, Son. I know. Maybe I should set a better precedent before I hand things over to Lampert."

Ugh. I can't stand Jaren Lampert. He's such a suck up. My father's second in command has never been a favorite of mine. He understands little of kindness, yet he knows much of how to overextend the power of his badge.

It's as if my father can read my mind. "Not sure I want Jaren following in the footsteps of a man who yells at a civilian who's asking for help." He sits back in his chair. "I'll, um, I'll be retiring soon, and I'd like to leave on a high note. You can expect better from me from here on out, Son."

It's a shock that hits me just as hard as it hits Rome. "What?" we say in unison. I'm not sure what surprises me more: the humility or the retirement announcement.

"You're retiring?" Rome asks, concern painting his

features. "Maybe we should start bringing Officer Lampert in on our weekly chats."

"That's a good idea. Eventually, though. Lampert doesn't know yet." The sheriff chuckles without a trace of humor. "I didn't know that's what I'd be doing until I said it just now. But it's time. It's time for new ideas. Mine got us here, and I don't like this place we landed." The sheriff sits back in his seat but doesn't let go of my hand.

I don't get it. We don't even hug. Now he's holding my hand?

My heart pounds with uncertainty. Why is my father being weird? I came out here with the full expectation he would tear me apart the second I intervened. I have nothing in my arsenal to combat against his niceness.

Rome nods. "I can keep it to myself. Colette is right, Elias. I do respect you. It's the only reason I ever ask anyone for help."

The sheriff nods once. "Then I guess it's time I make myself more respectable. Your mother..." My father pauses, swallowing hard because Mama Valentino is the one topic none of us are stupid enough to bring up. "She would be proud of you for asking for help. And she would be ashamed of me for treating you the way I have. I respect you, Son. I really do. I'll be better at showing it."

I stand, pulling my hand away because now I know something is wrong. An alien abduction would make more sense than my father saying anything so thoughtful. He's never said half those things to his own kids.

Rome stands abruptly, putting on his sunglasses because I just surmised a hint of raw emotion stripping away the stoic demeanor in his beautiful blue eyes.

I catch a glimpse of his ring that all the Valentino men wear with their family's crest emblazoned in the gold. In that simple piece of jewelry, I see the pride that runs deep in the men in their family.

"I appreciate it, Sheriff. Miss Kennedy." Rome's voice breaks on the last note, so he turns and stalks away, Orlando in his shadow.

I'm standing in front of my business, flabbergasted that I just witnessed something so surreal.

Even stranger, my father rises and opens his arms to me, inviting me in for a hug.

I don't know how to hug him. I can't even picture it in my mind. Maybe I could force myself to participate, but my feet won't push me forward. Would it mean that I forgive him for sending me away? Would it mean that we love each other?

Do I love my father?

I'm a deer in headlights, uncertain which way is safe, and which is a trap.

"Coco," my father beckons, his arms still outstretched.

My chest moves unevenly. "I... I don't know how to do

that!" I blurt out before dashing into my salon. I run to my office and lock myself inside, sinking to the floor.

Of all the things my father taught me, he never showed me how to hug him.

That is one lesson I know I am not ready to learn.

3

FRIENDLY PARK
ROME

I cannot relax here. There's an itch in my soul whenever I come near this particular stretch of the West End. It's supposed to be restful and fun, but it is nothing short of depressing. "This place is gray. Gray and brown. There's nothing that makes me believe there's life worth saving in this whole square mile."

Orlando is used to my rants, so he waits this one out. He doesn't sit on the park bench, nor do I. The thing is littered with graffiti and bird poop. I don't mind getting the occasional blood splatter on my clothes, but sitting on that bench would be crossing the line of what I can tolerate.

I motion to the grocery store on the other side of the "park". "Bars on the windows, crooked signage, and the place stinks of halluci-blend. No one wants to shop in there."

Orlando stands near a swing set that has only one

useable swing. "You want me to have a talk with the owner?"

I shake my head. "It won't do any good. If they could do better, they would. But why bother?" I motion around to the playground equipment that is easily three decades old. "Nothing in this end of the city is worth fighting for."

Orlando studies the one working swing with an inscrutable expression tightening his features.

He keeps his thoughts to himself, whereas I am content to rant like a lunatic to my cousin and best friend. I grip the edge of the merry-go-round that doesn't even spin properly anymore. "I want a city worth fighting for. I want us to take pride in who we are. No one will take us seriously if we don't set the standard."

Orlando sighs. "So, what? You want the crew to fix up the playground? It would be a nice night off from sniffing out drug dealers."

I shake my head, grinding my teeth because that's what I do when I am too frustrated to make sense. "No. It's more than that. More than this. It's an internal job. If I fix this up, it's not the whole fix. I want our people to demand more for ourselves. I want us to insist on a better quality of life, and then we work together to make that happen." I shake my head. "Just because the rest of the world doesn't respect us doesn't mean we can we give up hope. The future must be better than this."

Orlando isn't resistant to my words, but I can tell he is not as invested.

This is not the sort of thing I usually bother Colette with, but today I'm just turned around enough to take out my phone with the sole intention of letting her see the side of me that doesn't have all the answers.

I like being the man who reads to her, the man who talks about philosophy on the phone with her. I don't want to be this man who is mired in frustration, but if we're going to really do this, I don't want to dip my toe in.

She should have all of me or none of me. That way, if I am too much for her, she can have all the information up front and bow out gracefully.

Please don't bow out.

"Fancy hearing from you midday. Everything okay?" she asks. The mere sound of her delicate yet steadfast voice settles my disheveled insides.

She is pure magic; I am convinced.

"I'm not sure." When she starts asking rapid questions with increasing panic, I smile.

No one worries about me, except for Orlando and my little cannoli.

I cradle the phone between my chin and my shoulder while I roll down my sleeves to fend off the chill in the autumn air. "I'm physically fine. No one's hurt. I just have something on my mind I wanted your help figuring out. Or maybe I want to vent. I'm not sure. Either way, Orlando is sick of me, so now I've called to annoy you. Give poor Orlando a break from my whining."

She pauses before she speaks. I can hear the noise of the salon in the background. "I like that. Fire away."

"I'm standing in the middle of Friendly Park."

Her voice melts with nostalgia. "Oh! The one with the metal slide that burns your butt on the way down in the summer?"

I glance up at the piece of equipment she indicates. "That's the one."

"I love that park. We all used to go there after family dinners, remember?"

My heart tugs in my chest as I picture my sweet little cannoli on the swings that are no more. "I remember. But I'm not sure you would recognize it now. It's a disaster, trésur. An absolute mess. The whole place is in need of repair. It hasn't been updated in decades. Graffiti. Garbage. It's sad. What are kids supposed to play on? What kind of life is this for them?"

I hear the close of a door and the background noise of the salon fade to nothing. Coletta's voice lowers, her tone laced with need. "Are you trying to turn me on so badly that I drive over there right now and jump your bones? Because hearing you talk so exquisitely? Knowing you care? A girl can only take so much."

Surprise tints my chuckle. "I actually did not intend that, but I'll tuck that fact away in my back pocket for when you're not working and can actually make good use of all that lust."

"Do you need help cleaning up the park?"

"I mean, my men can do it, but it's not about that. It's that the beautification funds for the West End are nonexistent. This park's state of disrepair wouldn't exist in the East End. The humans wouldn't stand for it. But we're just accepting that this is the best the world can do for vampires. We accept that we get table scraps while the world feasts. I want us to care. I want my people to stand up and demand more." I glance around at the patchy dirt and weeds that used to be grass. "Until we do, nothing will change."

Colette's heels click along her office floor. I love the sound of her heels almost as much as I love the sight of her wearing them. She emanates a calm power that inspires me to stand straighter and try harder. Though she is barely five feet tall, the way she carries herself makes her presence tower over most in any room she enters.

I love it.

She has that way about her. I want my people to feel that straightening of their spines.

Her voice soothes me. "You want to get to the heart of the problem, not just fix the outside. Am I hearing that correctly?"

I exhale, grateful she understands me so easily. Maybe

we really are the same. "Yes. I don't know where to start. It feels like a battle too epic to start fighting on my own."

"Then it's my turn to start doing some heavy lifting. Give me the afternoon, okay? Are you alone?"

"I'm with Orlando."

"Good. Hand the phone to my big sweetie pie."

I snort at her cuteness. "Can I please be there when you call him exactly that?" I hand the phone to Orlando, who raises his brows at being brought into our conversation. "Colette wants to talk to you—her big sweetie pie."

Orlando takes in a long breath before he answers, glaring at the phone as if it has farted in his face. "Yeah?"

I can hear Colette's charm mingling with her take charge attitude. "Orlando, did you know that you're my big sweetie pie?"

Orlando cringes. "I hated it when you called me that when you were little, and I hate it even more now. What do you want?"

"I want you to take Rome out for a few hours. Anywhere to get his head cleared and his blood pressure lowered."

"What?" Orlando looks less than pleased about having to care about my blood pressure. "Vampires don't have to worry about human diseases, Colette. His blood pressure is fine."

"Please, Orlando. Give me a few hours to work on the park problem. Take him somewhere that isn't work and that isn't the park. Do something good for yourselves for a single afternoon. Please?"

Orlando scowls at me for giving him the phone. "I am not taking orders from you."

Colette's voice turns sharp. "Why are you such a bull-headed man? If I told you I needed you to bash someone's head in, you wouldn't hesitate. But asking you to take a few hours to enjoy your lives is suddenly where you draw the line? If Rome wants the world to change, then you two have to start. You are always working and never enjoying. I can help you with this, but you have to be willing to bend."

Orlando shoves the phone back into my palm. "Handle your woman. She's talking nonsense."

Yep, Colette heard that. I cringe because I know exactly how well his words are going to go over.

Her voice shouts into the phone. "Handle me? You want to rethink your words, you jackass? I don't need to be handled. You are the most stubborn mule I have ever met, Orlando! Have fun for three hours, or I swear, I will make your life miserable!"

I cannot keep the smile off my face, though I know I should be frustrated that my cousin and my girlfriend can't talk for more than a few sentences without getting into it. "Okay, tré-sur. We'll take the afternoon off. What do you have up your sleeve?"

"A surprise for you and a middle finger for your cousin. Tell my big sweetie pie to play nice."

She ends the call, leaving me with more questions than I had before we spoke.

I turn to Orlando. "I think we're supposed to be having fun right now."

Orlando shoots me a wry look, as if to ask if I have lost my mind. "I don't have the faintest idea how to do that."

"Neither do I."

It is then that realization hits me like a gong. I want the West End to be better, but I have no idea how to enjoy my own life. I don't know how to have fun.

How can I fix a playground if I don't know how to play?

4

THROWING THE GAUNTLET
COLETTE

It is normally no small feat to get a meeting with the mayor, but luckily, whenever I walk into any building, doors open that usually would remain shut.

It's time to use my macabre celebrity for the good of the people that my blood set out to kill.

Do I have time for this? Not really. Launching a new branch of my business is an all-hands-on-deck type of situation. Still, when Rome opened up to me about his aching heart for the vampire children in the West End, my schedule suddenly cleared.

This is not my most powerful outfit, but it will have to do. My pink silk skirt swishes over my thighs with every step that I take in my cream stilettos and matching blouse. With a pop of lipstick and my hair in a respectable ballerina bun, I am ready to attract the most attention I can muster.

People want to know what the Last Deadblood is up to? They're about to get an earful.

I have a list of news channel heads on my phone, so I called them all on my way over here after giving the mayor a fifteen-minute heads up that I am on my way and require his attention.

My father is also summoned to come, but I give him the full explanation, ending it with a succinct, "I don't care if you approve, Sheriff. This is what I want to do. I think it would be good for the precinct if you stood behind me on this. If you're in, meet me at Friendly Park in an hour, prepared to make a statement."

I hang up before I get his response.

I don't want to hear it. I don't want him to talk me out of trying to make the world a more accepting place. Tolerance is not the same as acceptance, and my people have been poor performers at both. I don't want my father to talk me out of fixing up the playground I used to run around in when I was a little girl.

I don't want him to tell me I am too sick to handle the stress that being a public figure puts on a person.

I already am a public figure, just for being born the way I am. Might as well put it to good use and do something I can be proud of.

Yes, there are better ways to handle this, but I am

unwilling to wait another day to address a decades-old problem. I've been silent long enough.

My mother was a diplomat. She advocated for change, pushing for tolerance and vampiric rights. I don't know everything about how she conducted herself, but I'm guessing it was with more preparation than this.

Still, I know myself. When I have a fire lit under me, the best time to move is that exact moment.

So here I go.

I smile at the straight-laced receptionist, giving him a little wave of my fingers as I walk past his desk and straight into the mayor's office, ignoring his "Um, excuse me, Miss. The mayor will be with you in a moment."

The mayor has had long enough to address the many issues he ignores.

I fling open the mayor's door, fixing him with a calm, collected smile that tells him he is either going to love working with me, or he is going to have to fake loving it. I don't much care which option he chooses, at this point.

"Hello, Mayor Stapleton. I can't believe this is the first time we're meeting." I shut his receptionist out of the office and measure up the seat across from the mayor.

The guest seat is shorter than his chair.

The jerk. I'm not about to accept the lower position of power in this negotiation. I am here to be heard and to walk out of here with a win. So I stand across from him, his messy desk between us.

The mayor stands, flustered but recovering quickly, as any politician worth his salt would do. "Good to meet you, Colette."

"Madam Deadblood," I correct him, coming up with a preference on the fly. I have many nicknames from the press, but that one always struck me as formidable.

He nods and runs his hand over the bald spot atop his head. He sucks in his pooched belly as he offers me the chair I absolutely will not sit in. "Madam Deadblood, have a seat."

Though he is in his late fifties, I will not be the child in our exchange. "I'll stand. This won't take long."

"Very well. To what do I owe the pleasure?" His expression is flustered, but pleasant enough. "I admit, I wasn't anticipating a meeting with you."

"Life's full of funny surprises, isn't it. Like Friendly Park in the West End. Have you been there recently?"

His head tilts to the side. "I can't say I have."

"Oh, good. We're going there next. I'd hate to take you to a place you've just been."

The mayor sits back in his seat, his fingers folding over his rounded belly. He is wearing khakis and a white polo shirt, looking like he is ready for an afternoon of autumn golf, rather than a day at a neglected playground. "What's this about, Madam Deadblood?"

My eyes fix on him. Even though I have a breezy smile

on my face, I know my eyes cast a wicked aura in his office, changing the atmosphere from lazy and self-important to finally alert. "Funny thing. I leave for a measly ten years, and the park I used to play at as a little girl is completely trashed. I have a trust from my mother, but I haven't touched it. So I'm here to give you a choice: either you allocate funds to help fix up every single park in the West End, or I take the money out of my mother's trust to do it. Either way, a human is going to take responsibility for this mess, since we created it by treating the vampires as sub-humans."

The mayor blinks at me. I can picture him stalwartly gluing his round bottom to his seat that much more firmly to protest any action on his part. "Is that so? I suppose you think humans sneaked into the West End to vandalize the vampire park. No, Madam Deadblood. The vampires broke it; they can fix it."

Pure evil crosses my features. I wasn't so naïve as to expect his immediate compliance, so I am ready to flash my teeth.

The mayor visibly backs away.

Declan calls it my Wicked Witch on a Mission face.

"Actually, we broke the park when we broke them. You have no right to take their tax money and ignore them with it. That money is supposed to serve them."

Mayor Stapleton holds up his hand, as if he has the right to educate me on an issue he willfully ignores. "It's supposed to serve all of Mayfield. Pumping money into a lost cause doesn't serve anyone."

I straighten, gathering my gumption because I anticipated this would be his attitude. "Very well, you had your chance. I look forward to the massive funds you dump into your futile reelection campaign in two years. It would have cost you less to put money into the West End, but that's your choice. I didn't expect your shortsighted nature could be remedied with a conversation."

"Excuse me? You're going to run against me?" He chortles at the notion.

"Of course not. I am merely going to tell everyone that the Mayor of Mayfield has left the citizens of the West End to fend for themselves."

He crosses his hands over his belly with a smug look to him, the charade of politeness gone. "Who do you think elected me? I represent the frustration Mayfield feels at having this blight on our name. They don't want funds taken away from thriving communities to be dumped into vampire territory."

I am unphased at his blatant display of racism. I expected as much. My smile has a malicious quality to it because I didn't want to step into my mother's stilettos, yet here I am. I wanted to be a businesswoman, not a diplomat.

But this is what must be done.

I can run my business and dip my toe into activism.

This is a one-time thing. I will help fix the parks in the West End and that's that.

I lean my hand on his desk as I angle my body toward him, not backing down. "Actually, you represent the ugliest parts of them. You are the part that they don't look at in the mirror because it's disgusting and embarrassing. You made it acceptable to be horrible. No one wants to think of themselves as a bad person, so they chose you to bear the weight of their secret shame."

I leave him to his spluttering as I walk to the door, fisting the handle. "I am leaving from here to go to Friendly Park. My mother will get all the credit for helping the children of the West End. I've got a dozen or so reporters waiting for me there. They will all hear that the mayor offered zero help to the citizens he takes money from." I straighten at the gauntlet I've just thrown. "You can either lead the way toward a better future for us all, or you can be the dead weight that gets cut off in two years when the world has outgrown its use of you." I point to the clock on his wall. "You have half an hour before I hold my press conference at Friendly Park."

He casts me a look of feigned boredom, but I know he is spooked by my threat. "You can't be serious. This isn't how this sort of thing is done, Madam Deadblood."

I snarl at him. "Oh, I know exactly how it's done. Children hurt themselves on poor equipment and you do nothing. People ask for help and you give them judgment and lectures. Vampires start to accept that this is who humans are." I fix him with my most intimidating glare, filled with the power that comes from wielding a weapon as strong as my mother's blood. "Do not underestimate my mother. Even from the grave, she can take away your career and leave you to ruin, or she can put you at the forefront of a movement where everyone looks to Mayfield to see how they should behave."

I don't wait for him to respond. It doesn't matter if he is onboard or not.

The world needs to change, and I am about to push it forward—whether my people are willing to open their hearts or not.

5

HUMANS IN THE WEST END
ROME

Orlando and I are terrible at manufacturing fun. We went for a walk and talked about work until Colette called me and told me to meet her at Friendly Park.

I am more depressed now than I was before I took this mandated break.

Man, I'm old.

I expect the same deserted wasteland when I turn the corner with my cousin by my side, but what greets me is at least fifty humans congregating in the park, looking around like they can't believe they are here.

I can't believe it, either. What are they doing? No one comes to this park, except drug dealers.

Orlando cusses. "What did she do?"

"You think this is Colette's doing?"

He points to the crowd. "It's mostly reporters. Look at all the cameras. Of course they're here for Colette."

I don't know what to do. "Should we hang back? I've never seen this many humans in the West End at one time."

Orlando nods. "Let's watch from here."

I point to Coletta's sedan. "There she is." My brows pinch together. "Is that the sheriff?"

Sure enough, when the cop car pulls in, tightening my stomach, the sheriff emerges, waving at the reporters and beelining for his daughter.

The two interact like business associates. Even from this distance, I see the stilted body language and the formal head bobs.

I remember her running into my dad's arms all the time. She rode on his shoulders and made him dance around whenever her favorite song came on.

I wonder what happened between the sheriff and his daughter that they regard each other so formally.

As if she can sense my study of her, Coletta catches my gaze and waves us over.

I don't like that all eyes are on me. I don't relish being stared at like a zoo animal in my own hometown. Still, I keep my gait loose and my spine upright as we stroll toward her.

Colette's face is tight with displeasure as I approach. "This park is a joke. I'm sorry, Rome. I didn't realize it was this bad."

"You've been away for a decade, Colette. How could you have known?"

"I've been back long enough. I had no idea. I will fix this." She reaches out to hold my hand but catches herself before she makes contact. She tucks her hands behind her back and lifts her chin. "Consider the West End parks taken care of. It's off your shoulders, okay?"

The sheriff is mute but watching his daughter carefully, so I examine my words before they come out of my mouth. "What do you mean?"

"I mean we failed you. Thank you for bringing it to my attention. This isn't your job; it's Mayfield's responsibility to care for its people."

I wrestle with the lump in my throat that keeps me from responding.

Coletta doesn't need my permission or thanks. She nods once with a firmness to her jaw and turns on her heel, making her way to the busted merry-go-round I used to pull her and Nico on when they were children.

Though the ground is uneven, she doesn't falter in her high heels. Her pink silk skirt flaps in the autumn wind like a flag marking the way to a brighter future.

She looks like her mother—calm yet determined to use her celebrity to force the world to care, whether they want to or not.

"She looks like her mother," the sheriff says aloud from

his spot beside me, as if he can read my mind. "I hate that she's doing this, but on the other hand, I couldn't be prouder."

"What exactly is she doing?"

The sheriff chuckles. "She didn't tell you? Buckle up, Valentino. The Last Deadblood is taking her rightful place in the world. If she is anything like her mother, the best thing we can do is either back her up or get out of her way."

It is clear to me that the sheriff loves his daughter, even if he must do so from a distance.

Coletta grips the rusty bar on the merry-go-round. My grimace matches hers as she steps onto the tilted steel disc that is supposed to be level to the ground. She smiles at the press, but it's not the adoring way she looks at me. She has an agenda, and she is using her beauty to make sure she has their attention.

Good, I say silently to her. *Use every weapon in your arsenal.*

My stomach is in knots because I don't like when she jumps out of a burning plane without a safety net. I should be by her side, but I know that if I go over there, people will be disgusted at the notion of the two of us dating.

Then again, we could probably be having sex in the middle of the park, and still, no one would believe a human would dare be with a vampire.

I shouldn't be thinking of sex with Colette when her father is right beside me.

I straighten, waiting for the crowd to settle as all eyes and cameras are trained on the most stunning creature in existence.

Colette's posture is perfect, her voice clear and commanding. "Thank you for coming. I've been away from Mayfield for ten years, but now that I'm back, I have some apologizing to do."

What the heck is she talking about?

Her chin is raised as she speaks. "See, I knew there were problems in Mayfield, but I didn't think they were mine to fix. I'm kind to vampires. My business is one of the few in Midtown that allows them entry. That should be enough, right?" She shakes her head and smacks the flat of her hand on the bar of the merry-go-round. "Wrong."

Orlando hisses. "If she cuts herself on that rusty thing, I swear..."

Colette rolls her shoulders back as cameras flash. "I used to play in this park, back when I was younger and so was the world. There wasn't as much stigma about vampires and humans coexisting back then as there is now. My father—your sheriff—took Fintan, Declan and myself here nearly every week to play with the Valentinos." She glances around sadly. "Only it didn't look like this. My father wouldn't have tolerated me playing here." She motions to the empty equipment. "See, I knew this would be a good place to talk to you all, because the vampires in Mayfield wouldn't tolerate their children playing on such unsafe equipment, either. They love their children just as my father loves his."

She has a funny look on her face, like she doesn't want to give a halo to her father but has to for the public.

It is clear to me she does not believe her father loves her.

"I need to apologize to the whole of Mayfield because I've been living here for several months already, yet I have done nothing about this park, or any of the parks in the West End. I thought the mayor would handle it, or I didn't think of it at all, because it didn't directly affect me." She lowers her chin a slight inch and presses her fist to her heart. "Such selfishness. My mother would be ashamed of me."

I hate myself for putting my problems on her. I didn't want her to feel any of that. Did I saddle her with my dissatisfaction?

I am in awe of this woman, and simultaneously annoyed that she is our lone ally.

I turn to the sheriff, keeping my frustration quiet. "Why can't you be like that? Why is it hard to get even an inch of progress from you?"

The sheriff's gaze hardens, his eyes still trained on his

pillar of a daughter. "Because I'm lost, Rome. I don't believe the world can get better, so I let it be what it is."

Despite the humility in his reply, I don't back down. "You're part of the problem, you realize."

He points to his daughter, who is detailing her plan for the press. "I see that now." He turns and shakes my hand. "I can do better. I'm not dead yet. I can still turn this thing around."

I want to take him at his word.

But for now, we watch Colette, crossing our fingers that the future shines brighter than the sins of the past.

Colette is a force unto herself. "The parks in the East End are lovely and safe, yet we live in the same city, so I know the funds are there. I am calling upon the mayor of the city to do something about these parks. I am asking him to stand up and put a stop to the idea that we are a city divided. That we are a people of have and have not." She grips the pole. "Children are children. We may have forgotten how to play, but they deserve the chance to redeem us all. If the mayor won't take care of the children of Mayfield, my mother will."

Orlando is transfixed. "What is she talking about? Has she gone mad? Mama Kennedy is dead."

Colette speaks above the confused murmurs. "My mother left me a trust that I haven't touched because I didn't know what to do with it. If the mayor refuses to care for the citizens he has sworn to serve—all the citizens, regardless of race—then I will use a portion of my mother's trust to fix up the parks. If Mayor Stapleton will not care for Mayfield, my mother will."

The sheriff nods in my direction. "That's my girl, and that's my cue." He leaves my side and trots toward her, sharing the spotlight as one who is used to delivering news to the public. "My daughter is right, and the police of Mayfield are behind her. My officers are prepared to volunteer as labor to help fix up the parks. We haven't protected the children of Mayfield as we should, and this park proves it."

I am rarely stunned, but my mouth hangs open in utter flabbergast at the sheriff's display of humility.

"Is this real?" Orlando asks in a pained whisper.

Colette's smile changes to something less than cheerful. She looks vindictive right now, like she is ready to skewer someone alive.

I follow her gaze and see that she is focused on a car that just pulled into the lot. Her voice lifts, turning every head toward the newcomer. "Ladies and gentleman, Mayor Stapleton would like to weigh in."

Orlando takes a step forward, his fists clenched at his sides. "What is he doing here? The mayor doesn't visit the West End."

The mayor walks through the crowd and joins her in the center of the trashed playground. "Good afternoon, everyone. I see Madam Deadblood got started without me. I am happy to tell you all that when she brought the state of this park to my attention, within the hour, I moved things around and am prepared to allocate funds to have every single park in the West End renovated to better serve the children of Mayfield."

I can tell he is expecting applause, but it doesn't come.

One brave reporter speaks up. "Mayor Stapleton, what were you waiting for? Are you only just now being made aware of the problem?"

Even though I know the reporter himself is only just now caring about the issue because Colette has forced him to, it is clear that the public will start distancing itself from outright bigotry if the Last Deadblood so wills it.

The mayor grimaces, but Colette takes over for him. "My mother would be happy to partner with anyone who prioritizes the children of Mayfield, no matter how late they are to the party. Thank you, Mayor Stapleton. I can tell this is the start of you going from being a tolerated politician to a man who is truly beloved."

She doesn't believe a word she is saying, but dang, if it isn't fascinating to watch her in action. I am utterly transfixed by the power of her beauty.

"She's crazy," Orlando muses.

"She's incredible," I counter.

If I was not mesmerized by this woman before, I know I

will never be the same after seeing her own her passion like this.

She loves me, no matter that she took back that declaration the second she uttered it to me. She is protecting my city.

This is love.

6

LILIES AND WARNINGS
COLETTE

I am exhausted. I wonder if this is how my mother felt after a long day of trying to convince adults not to be spiteful and selfish.

Yet even though I am my mother's daughter, I am still my own woman. She was the diplomat, while I am the business owner. Dipping my toe into both ambitions means the last two days were spent coordinating the parks' cleanups and rebuilds.

My inbox is full. Even as I pace my office well after my stylists have gone home, the machine of long overdue progress is still droning on and on.

My to-do list is growing, but I try not to let it drain me. It's perfect timing, really. As the sun sets in Mayfield, the workday is just beginning over in Lonmure. Everyone is so sophisticated over there with their accents and pastries. They like to think the problems of inherent bigotry don't affect them. They don't realize that over time, their raised noses are hardening their hearts against an enemy of their own making. Most people outside of Mayfield will go their whole lives never meeting a vampire, yet they still have opinions.

Vampires aren't allowed to fly, so that's that. The rest of the world has only television to help them form their opinions of the minority race.

I toe my shoes off, groaning at the ache in my feet to which I have long since grown accustomed. While I would love to go home and sleep, I know that is not an option.

With my last two days spent on vampiric rights and shaking down Mayor Stapleton for loose coins, I am certain I will be here at least another hour—and that's if all my phone calls go smoothly to my branch managers overseas.

I am behind on making shampoo.

I need to outsource that. I've known I've needed to for some time. I have an employee overseas who keeps the supply plentiful for my salons there, making more shampoos and conditioners using my signature recipe for the salon.

The Kennedy Salon in Mayfield is still new, so I haven't hired someone to take that over at the Midtown location yet.

One thing at a time.

I drag in a deep breath and start on my phone calls,

checking in with my branch managers as I pull up the monthly reports I was supposed to review earlier today.

So glamorous.

I need to hand this task off to someone. A business manager would be fantastic, but I'm still a new franchise, and I don't want someone doing this wrong.

Not like I am certain I'm doing this right. Still, if a mistake is made, I want it to be my mistake.

An hour later, I feel no closer to the end of my to-do list. In fact, with each phone call I make, the list only seems to grow, because my managers need support with a few odds and ends.

It looks like I might be sleeping here tonight.

Declan thought my choice of a futon in my office was an odd piece of furniture, but I know myself. If I need to get something done, I'm not going home until it is finished.

When my phone rings, I answer without looking at the caller ID. "Yeah?"

Rome's sexy voice is a welcome distraction. "I'm guessing it's poor form to break into your business. Mind letting me in?"

My smile breaks the rhythm of my workflow. "Not at all."

I pad through my business in bare feet. The space outside my office is lit only by a dim floodlight, ensuring I don't bump my toes on anything. I end the call as I open the backdoor, welcoming the most beautiful sight in the entire world into my salon well afterhours.

My boyfriend looks like he's got a million things on his mind, yet he is here for reasons I have yet to understand. Nighttime is usually his busiest, so I'm not sure why he's driven clear out of the West End and landed himself at my salon this late at night.

His mouth is firm. His eyes burn with an intensity that tells me something is very wrong, indeed.

Still, Rome is breathtaking. Holding a bouquet of lilacs and lilies? I am powerless to deny him anything. "For the queen of the vampires," he says with no hint of a charming smirk.

"That's quite the title. I think most vampires would disagree. But I'll take it tonight, mostly because I'm too tired to argue, and you come bearing gifts."

Our phone call last night was rushed because I had so much to take care of. I can see now that he's been dealing with yet more issues that I could have been helping him get through.

We'll talk about it all.

But first, we kiss. I don't know any other way. When Rome is near, I forget the basics, like normal conversation. I want to be in his arms, pressed up against him so I can feel the irregular thrum of his heart. The moment the door shuts behind him and locks, I lean up on my toes and kiss his supple lips.

There's my Rome. Rigid as he was, now he is soft and pliable as my arms wind around his neck. I have to stand on my tiptoes and he has to bend his knees. Lilacs brush the base of my neck as he melts into the kiss, sucking on my lower lip the moment my knees weaken for him.

Always for him.

Only for him.

Then abruptly, the kiss stops, and Rome is standing a foot away. "I didn't come here for that." He runs a hand through his thick obsidian hair, flustered that I took what I wanted when he clearly came here with a mission.

I touch my lips, savoring the cinnamon taste of him even after it's gone. "Sorry. I forgot myself for a minute. What's going on? You've got that look about you."

"What look?"

I point to his pinched brows and the tightness of his mouth. "That face that says you're not going to sleep unless you talk something through." I motion for him to follow me. "I'm doing a bit of paperwork in my office. Come on back and tell me all about it."

"Coletta," he says, but nothing else comes.

I turn but realize after two steps that he's not following. I pivot to reevaluate his uncertain gaze aimed at me. "Is everything okay, Rome?"

He leans against the door, his head tilted back. "How can you ask me that?"

Now it's my turn to frown. "Did something happen

since I saw you last? Whatever it is, I'm not in the know."

Rome stares down at the petals in his hands, as if he is speaking to them and not to me. "*You* happened."

I quirk an eyebrow at him, feigning interest instead of the worry I am beginning to experience.

Did I do something wrong?

"Explain," I say, freezing in my tracks.

Rome shakes his head. "I thought I was the only crazy one, but I'm not. You're just as crazy as I am when you care about someone."

I frown at him. "That had better be a compliment."

"It is. Or, I think it is. Maybe it's a warning. I have to give those to myself all the time."

All breath leaves my lungs. If he is breaking up with me again, this time with flowers, I swear... "A warning for what?"

"A warning that I'm me, and all that entails. You're attaching yourself to a man who's never had a relationship last more than a few months. I have no interest in dating because I know myself. If I'm in, then I'm all in. I'll move heaven and earth to make the person's life better." He leans back again and bangs his head against the door in a slow rhythm. "That's what you did for me. The flowers are supposed to say thank you, but I'm not deserving. The West End is my problem. The vampires are my people." He motions between the two of us. "I'm not used to a woman taking care of me the way you do."

I start to regain my optimism that Rome is not going to get spooked and run out on us, but you never know, so I keep my movements to a minimum. "Warning received. Now here's yours: I am me, and all that entails. You're attaching yourself to a woman who understands herself. If you tell me you're having a problem, and I'm upset about those same things, then I move on it. You might have to get used to that part of me." I motion around my business. "I'm not in the mood to slow myself down just because it makes sense to take things at a normal pace. I'm not interested in normal."

He hands me the bouquet, but the warning is still clear in his eyes. "Be careful. I might be bad at this. At us."

I take a long inhale of the flowers, letting the powerful fragrance and the gesture fill my senses. "I'm not interested in careful, either."

At this, the corner of Rome's mouth quirks. "You don't say."

I twine my fingers through his when I hear my phone ringing. "Come on. I'm still working. I haven't seen your face in two days."

Rome chuckles, his shoulders finally relaxing now that he's done his part to try and convince me he would make a dreadful boyfriend. When we get to my office, he takes in the scope of the mess on my desk with wide eyes. "You're busy, I see. Anything I can help with?"

I hold up my finger as I answer my phone. "Yeah?"

One of my branch managers is having trouble with the bottle supplier. She wants to switch to another kind.

"We've been down that road before, and it was a disaster. I'll call them now." I end the call with my branch manager and pull up the number for my bottle supplier.

Rome rubs the nape of his neck. "You're calling a vendor now? It's ten o'clock at night."

I wink at my boyfriend as he unbuttons his cuffs and rolls them. "He's in Lonmure. It's not even midday there."

"Ah. How can I help?"

I tilt my head in his direction. "You don't want to help with my business. It's all boring behind-the-scenes stuff."

He sends me a crooked smile from the other side of my desk. "Hello, I own several restaurants, landscape companies and business strips. I can handle the boring stuff just fine."

I can't picture Rome stressing over minute business discrepancies, but the visual is amusing, I must say.

For the next hour, I make phone calls while Rome balances my books, making sure everything is as it is supposed to be.

I'm sure there are sexier things we could be doing, but I can't think of a single one. Watching him work beside me on something that he has no vested interest in makes me want him that much more.

By the time midnight rolls around, I am exhausted but more attracted to him than ever before. "How is it you look positively delicious with a pencil in your hand, fully clothed and all serious like that?"

Rome chuckles at my blatant flirt. "It's a gift. You should see me turn in our taxes. I'm devastatingly handsome those days."

"I have no doubt." I motion to the paperwork that is significantly less in bulk and far more organized. "You didn't have to do this, you know. I appreciate the help, but I know this isn't anyone's idea of a fun night."

He looks up at me from my chair and motions for me to sit on the futon. "You haven't stopped moving this entire time. You haven't sat down."

"If I sit, I won't want to get back up. I need to finish all of this. I'm a little behind with everything."

Rome's demeanor shifts as he stares up at me from the chair. He adjusts the ring on his finger with his family's crest emblazoned in the gold. "Why did you do it?"

I get the feeling he is coming to the crux of why he stopped by tonight.

He stares up at me with a mix of marvel and confusion. "I told you I was frustrated, and the next thing I know, you're driving to the park with the mayor and your father in tow."

I don't know how to answer him. I cannot tell if he's upset with my actions, or if he is still trying to figure me out.

I choose my words carefully. "Declan was bullied in

school."

Rome's head tilts at my abrupt change in topic.

I tug on my fingers as the story surfaces. "He went to Fintan, who told him to man up. He talked to my dad, who brushed it off like it wasn't a real problem." I shake my head. "They didn't do anything to help. I love Declan. So I did what I thought needed to be done. I hopped on my bicycle and rode to the high school. I found out which car was the bully's and slashed the tires with a steak knife. Sugar in the gas tank. Nothing too crazy, but enough to take the bully down a notch. Did that once a month until the kid graduated high school."

Rome covers his mouth to hold in his surprised chortle. "How old were you?"

I shrug. "Twelve? Old enough to know that my father or Fintan should have done something. But they didn't bother, so it was up to me to protect my family." I motion between us. "That's all this is. You were being neglected, so I took care of it. Doing nothing only suits me for so long before I start to get itchy."

Rome stands, his gaze connected with mine as he moves around the desk slowly and steps toward me. "Everyone knows about the problem, but no one does anything about it." He motions to my desk. "So consider me your secretary for the next... however long you need me. You blew me away. It's been two days, and already there's a plan in place and work is starting in the morning on the first park." Rome steps closer so he is only a breath away. His hand cups my cheek as he stares into my eyes. "You have no idea how powerful your support is to me. I'm not used to anyone but Orlando caring about what I want."

My hand reaches up to rest on the back of his. "I care. That's my park, too."

The corner of his mouth quirks. "I had no idea you cared about the park so much."

His mouth is close to mine, so close that I can smell his cinnamon breath. "I adore the park."

It's a bold statement because part of me is toying with telling him that I love him.

But when I did that the last time, it was a bad idea. Too soon. Too strange.

I trace his lips with my thumb. "If something is bothering you, then I will take care of it."

Rome closes the meager gap between us and kisses my lips, plunging my tired body in a pool of lust I am helpless to escape. I drown for him. I am always drowning, gasping for breath that only his handsome features grant me.

His hands brush over my cheeks, my shoulders and arms, then dip to the curve of my hips, where they find their own personal playground. Rome's hands explore my body as if he seeks to memorize every nuance I hide from the public. I am his hidden treasure, waiting impatiently to be explored and plundered.

Rome's lips are what poems are birthed from, so I don't

take them for granted. I taste them, savor them and self-ishly wish for more.

My body presses itself to his as I give up any pretense that I know how to navigate an infatuation this powerful.

Rome kisses me harder, then presses his forehead to mine for the span of a few ragged breaths. "I don't understand why you're being so good to me. You were really going to take money out of your mother's trust?"

The corner of my mouth quirks. "It was meant to be a bluff, but yes. If the mayor didn't comply, I was going to dig into the trust for it."

"I wouldn't have let you do that, I hope you know. When I told you my frustrations, it wasn't because I was hoping to take your mother's money."

I kiss him again, shushing his fretting. "I know. But she would be ashamed of me if I didn't do something. It's her legacy that's slowly being forgotten. I can't let that happen."

Rome kisses my forehead and then brings my head to rest against his chest.

Not too long ago when we were making out, we experienced a shock of some sort just when it was getting to the good part. It was a popping sensation that spooked us both, so we had to slow down.

We never spoke about it after it happened, but it's in the back of my mind whenever I kiss him with the intent of losing control.

I'm glad that spark of a shock didn't happen this time. Now I can hold him as close as I crave.

He waits until our hearts beat in a steadier, shared rhythm before he speaks again. He holds me to him, his thumb tracing my hipbone from back to front in slow circles meant to marry my pelvis to his.

His voice is quiet while my breathing grows loud. I try to act normal as he slowly undoes my decorum. I can think of about fifty positions I would like him in on my couch, but I hold back because I know he has something on his mind that isn't my overactive hormones.

He kisses my lips just once, as if I am not about to tear his shirt off so I can lick the firm planes of his chest. "I wasn't expecting you to solve my problem with the park, but I'm glad you did. Getting the mayor to pay for it? That was priceless. Now I can busy myself obsessing about the dry cleaner's, which I'm sure is the place where the halluci-blend is coming into the West End. Vampires' fangs are falling out the more addicted they become. It's not good, tré-sur. The halluci-mend my family makes is nothing like this. It gets you high and takes away any pain, sure, but it isn't addictive and there aren't lasting side effects like this." He shakes his head, letting his frustration spill out because I am his safe place. "Don't think it's escaped my notice that any drugs being pushed in the East End haven't been bastardized at all, but the stuff sneaking into the West End is deadly, addictive and dangerous."

I spread my fingers across his firm chest, loving the feel of his body. "I'm working on it, honey. I'll get to the bottom of who is doing this to your people. Give me a week."

He chuckles, no doubt thinking I am joking.

I am not. I've been narrowing in on a few things in my research. If Rome's gut is telling him that the dry cleaner's is where we need to go digging, then that's the spot.

I trust his gut.

I trust *him*.

That revelation rings through my body like a gong.

More than love, this one declaration might be the only thing that could make or break us. It's not something I grant often or ever, outside of Declan. But as I blink up at him in wonder, I realize that my heart has opened up in ways I never expected. "I trust you."

Rome knows exactly how sacred those three words are. He grips my hand over his chest. "I trust you, too." I startle when he swears aloud. "I'm not sure I've ever said those words before. At least not to anyone other than Orlando."

I lean up, nuzzling his nose with mine. "I am so much sexier than Orlando."

The corner of his mouth tugs upward. "Indeed. It's Orlando's one downfall." Then he kisses my lips, sealing our affection like a promise.

There is much we are still learning about each other. But for tonight, we settle on the solid truth that we have each other's backs, no matter what comes next.

7

DOOMED DATE
COLETTE

I don't want anything to do with Fintan's restaurant tonight. Once a month, I agreed to go on a blind date of my eldest brother's choosing, so I could consider continuing the deadly family line.

My retaliation is that I usually pick out a horrid date for Fintan, but I didn't have time to scout out anyone truly annoying, so Fintan is off the hook for tonight.

No such luck for me.

No one asked me if I wanted to have children. I'm not sure I have ever asked myself that question. It's a can of worms, really. Because no matter what the answer is, I know I cannot go through with it. If I have a girl, she will then be the Last Deadblood, and the world will have little chance at finding peace.

The deadly blood that can only be passed down through the women in my family needs to end with me.

Fintan has other plans.

I am wearing the same thing I worked in all day. I didn't bother going home to change or freshen up. If I have to go on this stupid date, I am going to make it clear that this will be the only time I see this gentleman, no matter how great Fintan tries to make him sound via text.

When my phone rings, I answer in a breezy tone.

Rome's voice greets me with none of the levity he had for me on the phone last night when we made jokes about our days. "Tell me to stay where I am. Tell me going into the East End is a bad idea."

I balk at the notion. "You know vampires aren't allowed in the East End. It's an old, outdated law, but it still stands. Whatever you need in the East End, tell me. I can get it for you."

Rome sounds strained, his cadence rough. "You. I need you. I know you have that monthly date Fintan set you up on tonight. I know that's where you're headed right now. Tell me not to go there and cause a scene, so the date ends sooner."

I grimace at his mindset. "You really don't want to do that. Honestly, it's not all that big a deal, Rome. These things barely last two hours. Less if the guy is a jerk."

"So I need to distract myself for two hours."

"That's a very good idea. In two hours, we can talk extremely dirty and flirty to each other on the phone."

"What's his name?"

I pause because I know this is going nowhere productive. "He doesn't have one."

"Good. Yes. The less I know, the better. Don't tell me. It will only drive me crazy."

I purse my lips, my voice quieting. "You knew this would have to happen. Unless we tell my family about us, I have to keep up the charade that I am single and willing to play ball."

"But you're not."

"But my family doesn't know that."

Rome sighs. "I'm overreacting. I know it. I hear how nuts I sound."

"Good, because I didn't want to be the one to break it to you. This is nothing, Rome. Less than nothing. It's an errand my brother needs me to run for his sanity."

Rome's tone darkens. "Because Fintan wants you to produce another Deadblood. He wants the humans to have an ace in the hole in case vampires actually get the courage to stand up for ourselves."

I swallow the shame that comes from knowing that Rome is spot on. "You don't have to worry about that. I will never marry and I will never have a baby. The bloodline will end with me. I just have to keep up appearances, otherwise my family wouldn't let me move back to Mayfield. I wanted to come home, Rome. This is part of that arrangement."

I can picture Rome's upper lip curling. "You are a

grown adult. You should be able to live wherever you want without archaic negotiations."

I don't tell him that my father had power of attorney for many years, so he very much had a say in where I lived.

That period of my life is behind me.

"Stay put. I'll call you in two hours." When I know that isn't enough to quell his angst, I add, "Ask my big sweetie pie to go out and do something fun. Orlando is good for you when you get cranky."

Rome scoffs. "I am a grown man. I don't get cranky."

"Really? Because you sound fussy."

Rome does not appreciate my teasing. "I told you I was no good at relationships. When I'm in, I'm all in, which means I don't take it well when my girlfriend goes on dates with other men."

My brows pinch together. "You know that's not what this is, though. We discussed this. You said you would try harder to be cool." I pull into the parking lot of the restaurant and turn off the engine. "Don't make this harder on me than it already is."

Rome pauses and then deflates. "I'm sorry. You're right. You told me this was how it has to be. I know. I'm being overbearing. Call me if it goes south?"

"The very second the date ends, I will call you."

After I tuck my phone away, my nerves ramp to an uncomfortable level. I take a pill, knowing I cannot get through this date without help.

I don't want to meet this man. Even as I walk into the restaurant and greet the hostess, I dread each step that directs me toward the table at the picture window in the front of the restaurant.

Fintan is an ass, who already called a number of reporters to alert them of my date. The man is talking with three of them, smiling with a mouthful of bleached teeth as he tells them all about his credentials.

"Yes, I got my doctorate last year. It's about time for me to settle down with someone special." Then he turns his chin and winks at me, as if that is a thing people do before they have been properly introduced.

Gross.

I do my best to ignore the questions the reporters ask me, answering only with menu options. "I think I'll treat myself to the steak tonight. Extra truffle butter."

The guy pulls out my chair for me, grinning at the cameras that snap photo after photo of the grand effort it takes to be a gentleman. One of the reporters coos when the man's hand brushes my shoulder.

My upper lip curls as I fix him with a glare. "No."

No explanation. No big lecture. Just a firm edict that he should not feel welcome to touch any part of me.

The man's smile falters as he takes his seat across from me. "It's a pleasure to meet you, Colette."

"Madam Deadblood," I correct him. We are not

friends. We are not on a real date of my choosing. We haven't even been introduced. "Hello, Mister Glumon."

"Artie. Call me Artie." He smiles with the artless charm of a television weatherman.

I motion for the waitress to come to our table. "Could I get the porterhouse, medium rare? I'd like extra truffle butter, too. That's all for me. Mister Glumon?" I cast across the table, wondering what the line is between disinterest and outright rudeness. I don't want to be a jerk to this guy, but I also don't want to give him the wrong idea that I am even close to interested.

Artie fumbles with his menu as the reporters give us the illusion of space. "I thought we would start with drinks first."

"I don't drink," I announce. I mean, that's technically true. I can have half a glass of wine, but I really shouldn't have much alcohol with my medication, so I steer clear altogether. At most, I will have half a beer when I'm out with Declan, and let him finish the other half.

"Oh. I didn't have time to look at the menu. What do you recommend?"

The waitress rattles off the specials, and Artie selects the meal of his choosing.

After the waitress leaves, Artie smiles at me as if I have said something amusing.

We are both aware that the cameras will be watching us through this entire ordeal.

"Tell me about yourself, Mister Glumon," I offer.

"Well, I have a doctorate, so you can call me Doctor Glumon, if you like." He casts an airy laugh my way. "I grew up an hour from Mayfield, so not too far from here. Now that my studies are finished, I actually have the time to settle down with someone. I've always been something of a go-getter. When I heard you were available, I sent Fintan the payment first thing."

I wasn't planning on actually listening to Artie's chatter, but that turns my attention fully on him. "I'm sorry, what payment?"

Artie waves off his words. "You know, the twenty grand to set this up."

I balk at him. "Excuse me? You paid twenty thousand dollars to be here? To date me? Who did you pay?"

But before I can hear his reply, I already know the answer. "Fintan arranged it. It's no trouble, you see. I come from money and made a killing in the stock market. I assure you, I have no problem securing you a future in which you will never have to worry about a thing."

My mouth is dry, and my soul feels rough like sandpaper. "Fintan is charging men twenty thousand dollars to go on a date with me?"

Artie's brows bunch together. "You didn't know that? I'll admit, I've never had to pay to take out a woman before, but I don't mind. It's you, after all. You're the Last Deadblood. As far as the elite go, you're it. I tend not to settle."

No wonder these dates are always a bust. Fintan is only doing this to line his pockets.

I flag down the waitress. "Could I get an extra steak to go after we finish our meal? And the lobster. And all of your sides and one of each dessert. I don't plan on cooking this week. And please put it on Fintan's tab. Tell my dear brother it's but a drop in the bucket of what he owes me."

The waitress nods, and I go back to my date. I smile and nod, acting as polite as possible while keeping the table between us as a buffer.

If I didn't despise Fintan before, I certainly do now.

8

DRY CLEANING
COLETTE

I really do need Wednesdays to run errands, but spending time with Rome is well worth cramming my errands into my lunch breaks during the rest of the week.

And this particular errand cannot wait.

The West End is dirtier than the East End. The media would teach us that the vampires are messier, that they don't care about their surroundings as much as humans do, but I know that's not true. Our taxes go toward beautification of the East End and Midtown, while there are several holes in the money trail that funds the West End.

Even though two of the three parks in the West End have been updated, the rest of the city needs some love.

One giant project at a time.

Before this past week, I hadn't driven through the West End since I had my learner's permit when I was fifteen.

There are pops of nature brightening the stretches of rundown commerce, but a tree placed here and there can only be expected to do so much. The buildings are in need of a fresh coat of paint, and the trash on the side of the road begs to be collected.

I can see why this side of town might make a person feel hopeless.

I pull into the parking lot, turning off my engine in front of the store my GPS directed me toward. There are four businesses on this strip, each one permeated with the mouthwatering scent of lamb from the grill place on the corner.

I had a plan this morning. Now I'm not so sure I am the person for this job.

When my phone rings, my fingers still on the car door handle, pausing my exit. "Funny you should call. I was just thinking about kissing you."

Rome chuckles. "Thank God you haven't changed your personality with no warning. I'm still not over your dad's one-eighty. Any clue what's going on with him? I know he said he would send police officers to help with the grunt work of fixing up the parks in the West End, but I wasn't sure he would actually make good on his word. I actually saw a vampire kid laughing with a police officer this morning. What is the world coming to?"

"I have no idea." I soften at the mental image of a

vampire child and a police officer sharing a moment of happiness. We need more of those.

"Your father said he was proud of me at our last meeting. My own father never told me that."

Mine never did either. But I don't tell Rome that.

"Now he's helping the West End fix up the parks? Every time I see a squad car in the West End, I immediately tense up, but now they're only here to fix the swing sets and pick up trash. It's still blowing my mind."

"My father being civil to you at your meeting is one thing I can't explain. But I pretty much strong-armed him into using the force to help out. So that's how we got there."

"It's more than that. You used your mother's memory. I think he'd forgotten her. You helped remind him of all that was good about his life."

I take that gem in and savor it. Perhaps my father is capable of love. Not for me, of course, but for his deceased wife.

I clear my throat. "What's on your mind, baby?"

"I never apologized for causing a scene in front of your business last week, arguing with your father in public. Utterly shameful. I want to make it up to you. Can I send you lunch?"

"That's sweet and totally unnecessary. I'm actually not at the salon right now. I'm running errands."

"I told you to let my assistant do that." I can hear the light scold in his voice.

"I don't mind. It's a nice change of scenery." My nose crinkles as Nino-bear's car drives down the street beside the parking lot of Martin's Dry Cleaning. "Did Nico get into an accident? His car is dinged."

"What? How do you know that?"

"I'm looking at it right now."

"He just left the house a few minutes ago." Rome's voice drops an octave. "Where are you, Coletta?"

My neck shrinks. "I'm running errands."

"Funny. I didn't know you had anything of interest in the West End. What's going on?"

"I'm not allowed to throw my human money into the West End to support vampiric businesses?"

I can tell Rome doesn't fall for my artful dodge. "Trésur, why are you lying to me?"

I grimace as guilt taps me on the shoulder. "I'm getting some dry cleaning done."

Rome swears. "I'm getting in the car."

"Don't bother. Seriously. I'm just dropping off some dry cleaning. I couldn't find anything in the books to substantiate your hunch, but maybe if I go inside and poke around, I'll figure it out."

"A hunch isn't worth you putting yourself in danger, Colette!"

My nose raises in time with my tone turning crisp. "I'm

hardly in danger. I'm dropping off dry cleaning in the middle of the day. It's nothing, honey. Honestly."

"I'll be there in five minutes."

"You will not. You'll stay put and stop worrying." Before he can get more worked up, I end the call and step with purpose and a smile into the dry-cleaning establishment.

Vampires are afraid of me, even though I've never hurt them on purpose. My face is widely known around the world because of my blood, so it's no surprise that the moment I enter, the redhead at the counter drops his sandwich onto his brown paper bag. He gasps and steps back as if I am fixing to rob him.

I hate scaring people by just existing.

I set my dresses on the counter and broadcast my brightest smile. "Hi, there. I was hoping you might be able to fit these into your rotation. And I'm sorry to bother you, but I'm extra finicky about the chemicals used on my clothes." I roll my eyes at my fabricated predicament. "Allergies. The worst, am I right?"

The poor vampire behind the counter doesn't know what to do with me. He stumbles through his response, rattling off a number of chemicals. I'm in so deep with my research that I can identify each item he lists and guess which companies from which they were purchased.

Nothing unusual there.

My mouth draws to the side.

I know Rome is not wrong. I trust his gut. I just haven't looked in the right place yet.

So I keep digging.

I smile at the man and glance at his nametag. "Well, thank you, Horace. That's very helpful. How long will these take to clean?"

He rattles off a date while I examine the pictures on the wall, pretending to be interested in the details.

"That'll work." When I glance at Horace, I realize he's got a jelly smudge on his cheek. "You've got something just there. Brown bagging it today, eh? I was thinking of stopping for lunch. Is the grill place on the corner any good?"

I know from the ledger that they order from Frank's Grill daily, enough for the entire staff and then some. Weird that the counter clerk is munching on peanut butter and jelly.

Horace shrugs. "I don't know. I've never been. I'm sure it's fine."

Something pings in the back of my mind.

I know I've landed on the crux of it all. I don't fully understand what I have discovered, but it's clear to me that this is where I need to continue my digging.

Horace motions to me. "You might want to go with a friend or something if you're headed there. We're in the West End."

I frown as if this is just occurring to me. "Oh. But humans are allowed in the West End, right? I'm not doing the wrong thing by being here, am I?" I cast him a friendly smile tinged with naïveté. "I've been gone from Mayfield for so long. Have they changed the rules since I was here last?"

As if the whole world as well as the sheriff's daughter doesn't know the rules.

I can tell he wants to add the word "Technically" before he says "No."

I don't belong here. I don't belong in the West End or near it. The trouble is, I don't belong in Midtown, either. And I've been abducted numerous times in the "safer" East End. People warned me about the dangerous vampires, but it's the humans who abducted me when I was a much younger target.

I don't belong anywhere.

My heart hollows at the thought I have never been able to escape. The revelation is nothing new, but it shatters my confidence all the same.

I thank Horace and turn on my heel toward the door, but just as I reach for it, I stop short at the intimidating presence filling my view on the other side of the glass. "Rome! What are you..."

But I know exactly why he is here.

9

SHOCKING KISS
COLETTE

Rome opens the door for me but doesn't make a move to enter the establishment. "Are you okay, Colette?" He braces himself in the entrance like he is about to scare the peanut butter out of Horace if the man merely looks in my direction. Rome's nostrils are flared, his shoulders tensed.

I don a pleasant smile as I step out into the autumn sunshine, trying to ignore what it does to me when he says my name with such passion. "Of course I am. I just dropped off my dry cleaning."

"In the car," Rome orders in a clipped manner.

My spine stiffens as I bristle, freezing on the sidewalk. "Try again."

Rome's chin lowers, his demeanor shifting from aggression to submission.

Well, he offers as much submission as a Valentino might ever be capable of exhibiting, anyway.

"Please, Coletta." He lowers his voice so Horace doesn't hear, even though I see in my periphery that the poor guy has escaped to the back. "We need to talk. I'm all worked up and worried. I want to get you out of here."

"That's better. Next time, add in a semi-believable 'Colette, I trust you.'"

"I do. I'm just…" He tilts his head to the side. "This is what I was talking about when I told you I can be over-bearing."

I motion to his tensed form. "And this is what I was talking about when I told you to try harder. I belong where I put myself. The dry cleaner's is a fine place for me to put myself for an entire five minutes. You can deal. Vampires aren't more dangerous than humans, Rome. I shouldn't have to lecture you about that."

I expect Rome to rise up against my anger, but surprisingly, he lowers his shoulders while his head bobs. "I should have listened better. Can we talk in my car?" He glances around because no doubt anyone seeing us standing together in vampire territory will do a doubletake.

"Okay. Just for a minute, though. I have to get back to the salon."

I follow him to his sedan and slide into the backseat, noting the buttery leather of the interior. It is no surprise that everything a Valentino drives is sheer luxury. I am grateful for the tinted windows that keep us from view.

"I'm sorry, tré-sur." Rome joins me in the back and threads his fingers through mine, bringing my knuckles to his lips. "You told me you were going into a business I don't trust without me there to protect you. Before I knew it, I was driving to you."

"What did you think was going to happen? Vampires never give me any trouble."

"I know that. But drug dealers aren't harmless, especially the ones cooking up halluci-blend. I know this dry cleaner's is involved somehow. Until I get to the bottom of this thing, I will worry if you set foot into that business. Please do me a solid and save me from having an ulcer."

I mull over his plea. "I can do that." I bring his hand to my lips for a quick kiss. My touch introduces ease back into his body, so much that he sags against his seat. "I didn't mean to worry you. I knew you were losing sleep over this thing; I figured I would be able to see the whole picture better in person."

He runs his free hand over his face. I can see he's tired. The skin underneath his eyes is purplish, and he has a lag to his movements. He shakes his head at himself. "You care about me, yet I snapped at you."

"Yes, you did. But that's behind us now. We have more important things to discuss." A smile plays on my lips. "I solved it. Well, I partially solved it. The dry cleaner's employees don't order from the grill on the corner for their meals, which incidentally, shouldn't be a business expense anyway. Daily lunch for your employees isn't a line item that belongs on the ledger, especially when the employee is eating a peanut butter and jelly sandwich he brought from home."

Rome frowns at the building, but when my verdict begins to click in his mind, he freezes, his mouth popping open as he processes my hypothesis. "Frank's Grill? That one there?"

"That's where I'd be digging if I were you. The dry cleaner's is involved, but they're just a stop along the way. They're not manufacturing the drugs. At least, none of the chemical companies they purchase from sells the ingredients they would need."

Rome balks at me. "How do you know what ingredients are used to make halluci-blend?"

I roll my eyes at him. "Hello, Fintan hung out with you while you made halluci-mend all those years ago. What we're tracking is a bastardized version of halluci-mend, so I'm guessing the ingredients aren't all that dissimilar. You used to make halluci-mend in the basement while Ninobear and I did our homework upstairs."

Rome scoffs, mildly impressed that I remember such things.

"Frank's Grill is your next stop. Hopefully your last, but you never know with these operations. They can go for miles before you hit the bottom and find the end of your trail." I kiss my fingertip and boop Rome's nose with it. "But at least we know where to dig next."

Rome's wide eyes examine the business on the corner, amazement still on his features. "I knew it. I knew something wasn't right." He shakes his head. "You talk like a sheriff's daughter who was raised around Valentinos. Trésur, thank you."

I lean over and kiss his lips just once. "If my baby can't sleep, that's a problem."

His neck shrinks when I dote on him. Dang, he's adorable. "I'm not your baby; I'm your old man." He flinches at his harsh verdict.

I shush his self-flagellation. "Hello, you're only thirty-five."

He motions to my body. "And you're twenty-five. Twenty-five and dating eligible men with degrees and whatnot."

I didn't tell Rome about Fintan selling me to the highest bidder. I haven't told Fintan I know about his side hustle, either. I can't wrap my mind around it all.

I don't want to focus on that. I want to be here, with Rome.

I love the look of our fingers linked together. "That date was over before it began. I'm with you. We're in this together, Rome. Remember that. The stress of the broken city isn't just on you anymore."

His thumb traces overtop of mine. He examines our joined hands with new appreciation, staring as if he has never seen anything so beautiful and simultaneously strange. "I think I'm starting to understand that finally. It's been a long time operating one way. I'm new at this."

"I can be patient," I promise, kissing his lips because they are begging for it.

Or perhaps I am the one doing the begging this time around.

I cannot stop kissing this man. I have to get back to work, but one more kiss turns into a cascade of affection. Though we are hidden behind tinted windows, I worry the world will find us out and tear us apart. It's all I can do not to tell him I love him all over again every time I see him.

Which would be foolish, because I would quickly take it back, like I did before.

Rome's fingers make a mess of my bun. He turns in his seat and drags me closer, squeezing whole chunks of my tresses so my head bends however he wants it. The extra stimulation makes me forget his moment of being over-bearing.

He pulls me to straddle his lap, which is a first for us. His groans are my favorite thing to collect as our passion heightens. He grips me tighter, driving the kiss deeper because that is what we both need.

How I crave this man. I spend much of my time admiring and respecting his steadfast spirit that is never devoid of a plan. But when I get a front row seat to Rome Valentino throwing the rulebook out the door so he can bruise my lips with his, those are the moments I know I will hold in my heart for as long as I live.

Everything about the way his hands caress and cup makes me ravenous for more.

The fervor builds as my fingers span his broad chest. My blue silk skirt fans across the tops of my thighs while my breasts press tight against my button-up white blouse.

This is the bliss of losing control.

I don't expect that same disarming popping sensation we experienced when we kissed not too long ago. It never happened again after that. But when it jerks us both, I know we need to slow down.

I don't know what it is, but it feels like nature's warning that something formidable is on the horizon.

The disconcerting pop is louder this time. It explodes on the inside of my body as well as from outside of me. It jerks me away from his kiss so much that my spine bangs on the back of the driver's seat.

"What the heck?" My eyes are wide while I catch my breath. "Did I shock you again?" I ask, knowing that's not something I should have to ask a man.

Rome's chest heaves as he rubs across his sternum in confusion. "Maybe. I can't tell if it's coming from you or from my insides. Either way, let's give it a second. That was... I don't know what that was."

My brow creases. "Why is it happening? Is that a vampire thing? Shocking someone's chest when you're about to tear their clothes off?"

Lust flares in his heated gaze as he takes in my words coupled with my disheveled state.

Now I know we are on the same page. The back of his car isn't an ideal place to ravish each other, but this is no longer a mere want I am entertaining; growing inside me is a need I cannot quench.

Rome's hands slide up my thighs as I settle closer to him on his lap, my thighs spread without an ounce of hesitation this time.

"I don't know what that was, but I do know that you can tear my clothes off whenever it pleases you." He leans his head back on the seat, his chest still jumping while he catches his breath. "Normally I would say it's the beginnings of the vampire mating ritual, but that's not what this is. It's not mating, because it's not possible for us to be mated." He closes his eyes. "I can be as close to you as we like without risking that."

I nod. "And being mated is a bad thing for a vampire."

Rome slides me closer to him. "Very bad. I would be a servant to you alone. I would forget the plight of my people, my own needs, and serve yours above all else. It gets very toxic very quickly. I can't afford that kind of weakness."

I gnaw on my lower lip. "Totally understandable. Then we

are a perfect match, since vampires can't mate with humans."
I hold tight to my independence with just as much ferocity.
The fact that we chose our relationship, rather than nature
forcing us to overly care about the other person is a relief.

His hand reaches around and skims my backside,
surprising a squeak from me. "Perfect, indeed. Come
closer."

My parted thighs settle more deliciously over his lap.
"Tell me more about mating," I ask him, my curiosity
battling with my libido while I kiss his forehead.

Rome nuzzles his nose across mine. "You would be
physically dependent on me. Think how much you would
hate me if that were true. You would have to drink doses of
my blood on a regular basis. Nothing would be as good
without me nearby. It's codependence at its finest."

I grimace. "Oh, gosh. I didn't know that part. That's
awful."

Rome is overworked. I can tell he's taking on too much
by the angsty edge in his kiss as his lips caress mine. He's
scared, which I didn't mean to do to him.

"Baby," I coo between kisses. "We don't ever have to
worry about that."

His lips are full and perfect, each kiss a delicious treat.
The noises he makes under his breath are an admission of
pain, and a need to place his worries somewhere safe.

I can be his safe person.

I trace his unshaven cheek, touching on the corner of his mouth as often as I like because he lets me access whatever part of him pleases me most in the moment.

Oh, how he pleases me.

We should slow things down. If his heart is having an adverse reaction to kissing me, that's something to be considered.

But when Rome's hands grip my hips, I know I am powerless to resist him. I will give him anything he wants, and what he wants is me.

"Are you okay?" I ask him as the lust begins to flare up in his eyes all over again.

"I will be." His kiss is harder this time, letting me know he is not about to slow things down just because his body is telling him to be cautious.

His hands roam where I need him most as his tongue plunders my mouth. His fingers slip beneath the hem of my blue skirt just so he can collect a gasp from my lips.

If he gets to do that, then I should be able to undo the buttons on his white dress shirt that hold his naked chest prisoner from me. There is no part of me that doesn't want to be pressed up against him, so I make quick work of opening up his shirt and tearing the fabric down his toned arms.

He rips his hands from his clothing so he can glue his fingers to the insides of my thighs. His tongue teases mine, turning this way and that while his fingers mimic the motion that sets my heart racing.

When his thumbs loop inside the silk of my underwear, that same physical shock hits us both again, breaking us apart. A cry of... not quite hurt, but definitely surprise... cracks out of me.

"It's fine," I say at the same time Rome commands me to "Get back here."

Our kiss explodes with passion the likes of which no shock from nature or the world can dull. I love what his fingers do to me, teasing and taking because there is no part of me I do not happily offer up to his capable hands.

My fingers bunch in his hair, tugging without mercy while my body makes it clear how needy it has been for his touch.

"That's right. Don't hold back," Rome urges, his fingers slipping to where they are most needed.

I want to kiss the parts of him that belong only to me.

All of him. Every bit of Rome belongs with me, even when he is dragging and worried. I'm not sure at what point my heart leapt out of my body and splattered across his face, but every time he is near, unless he is holding or kissing me, he is too far away.

I trekked across the city for him on a hunch.

Though I know I shouldn't have said it, there is no denying that I might never stop loving this beautiful man.

10

MY BIG SWEETIE PIE
COLETTE

was planning on coming in early to make shampoo once a month, guessing the products wouldn't be a hot topic in the salon this early on. I wasn't expecting my stock of shampoo to sell out this quickly, but yesterday three women came in after their styling last week just to purchase the shampoo, and I had to give them rainchecks.

I have a five-year plan, and I am falling behind on my pursuit of it, what with all this vampire rights business I've been doing on the side. I need to learn balance.

One thing at a time. Right now, there is no civil unrest inside my salon. There is only shampoo.

Everything is quiet inside when I am the only person in the place. It feels like my own personal cocoon. I don't like sitting in my chair in my office, so I plop my butt on the desk, spreading out my papers and concocting a to-do list long enough to put any sane person to shame. I need to call my vendors to make sure a few products get reordered, so I take care of that before I get started up in the kitchen.

I pride myself on making my own products and selling them out of my shop. I only put my name on things I truly believe in, so it makes me smile whenever I see my logo on the silver bottles.

Which reminds me, after this batch, I'll be running low on shampoo bottles. I need to order more.

I add that to my to-do list, and then get started on my shampoo. I wanted this space for the social statement it makes, of course, but this particular building has a kitchen in the back, which is perfect for making my hair care products. I am finicky about my independence, so when I knew I wanted to be a stylist, I decided to go all the way and create my own shampoo, too. This way, I will never be subject to a supplier and their potential drama or subpar ingredients.

I love the way the soap smells when it's heating up. I'm sure the inventor of the candy thermometer didn't envision their product sticking out of a pot of silky, shimmery viscous liquid.

One other thing I love about making my own products is that you can't rush the process. I have to slow down. I have to take my time, letting the soap heat gradually while I stir the thick liquid. I am in such a rush usually that I don't let my thoughts settle long enough for me to truly examine them.

But this is *my* time.

It's my time to process all that I cannot make sense of.

My father was nice to Rome. I don't know what that means or why it's happening, but I'll take it. I've been fighting for the peace treaty to actually mean something for so long; yet when my father acts kindly toward a vampire, I don't know how to take it. The whole thing is weird. Even though it's been two weeks since he started to do actual unbiased policework, part of me doesn't trust my father's enlightenment.

Man, I'm jaded.

I didn't used to sniff a gift from the universe before opening it. I remember being a goofy little girl who didn't care much about the adultish things I couldn't control. How I would love a small taste of that little girl's optimism. I readily trusted that everything would work out somehow. I grew up with one foot in the West End and the other in the East End. I never felt off-balance until I grew old enough to understand that the world was telling me I had to choose.

I have faith that Mayfield can be more than this divisive place with needless boundaries.

Maybe that little optimistic girl is still inside of me after all.

I turn on the station that always has the divas of the

sixties playing. The sound of their soulful beauty makes my hips sway in a slow rhythm, reminding me not to jostle the soap too much while I stir. I love the silvery sheen the soap has when it starts to come together. It's still got a few more steps, but every part of the process is relaxing to me and brings about something prettier than the stage before it.

Rome's face pushes into my brain without me conjuring his visage, causing me to drop the wooden spoon. It's not uncommon for me to daydream about the man who plays the main role in my musings, but this feels like an abrupt topic shift. Like being interrupted with no explanation as to why.

That jarring shock that happened when we were ravishing each other in the backseat of his car has left me unsettled ever since. What does it mean? Why did it happen? Should I be worried?

My shoulders tense as I adjust my grip on the wooden spoon. A feeling of dread washes over me, though I can't put my finger on why. It's as if I am certain, for no reason at all, that something is wrong with Rome.

Very wrong.

I shake my head at myself. I have no evidence to prove anything is perilous for Rome in this exact moment. He is no doubt sleeping, because he often works into the night and gets home to sleep around dawn.

The nagging feeling that something is amiss pushes

my fingers toward my phone, but I hold tight to the wooden spoon.

That's crazy. Nothing is wrong with him at all. He's sleeping. You're just not used to being in a relationship, so you're imagining the worst. You can be happy, Colette. Nothing bad is happening to him.

I go back to stirring, but the soap isn't as distractingly pretty as it was before.

I chide myself for being a pest, but ignoring my instincts isn't a habit I would like to develop. I don't text Rome, but call him, risking waking him for no good reason. I can picture him shaking his head at my worry, and the subsequent lecture that's going to come wherein he reminds me that being the head of the Valentino family comes with sizable risks and danger.

I'll have to invest in thicker skin if I want to keep up without driving him nuts.

My imagination is cruel. Rome would never talk to me in such a demeaning way.

He picks up on the third ring, his voice surprisingly alert without a touch of sleepiness. "Tell me you're okay."

I swallow my worry. "I was just going to ask the same about you."

I can hear men shouting in the background, which tells me Rome's night has been too eventful for him to turn in yet.

Rome's voice is strained. "Orlando's been stabbed."

Before I can react, more information chases in on the heels of the headline. "Some bastard punctured his lung."

A cold horror washes over me. Sure, vampires live through just about anything, but the fact that someone aimed their knife for his lung tells me they were hoping for a lethal hit through the heart. "They were aiming for his heart if they got his lung."

"Exactly. He's bleeding all over the place. I'm driving us out of the West End, so I can't help him." Then he calls I'm guessing toward the back of the car, his chin away from the phone. "Hold on, Orlando. I'll get us somewhere safe and then I'll help you. It's going to be okay."

If Orlando was stabbed in the West End, then it was a vampire who did it.

"Here," I say without thinking anything through. "Bring Orlando to the salon. I'm here now. I have a couch he can lie down on. I can lock the office so no one sees him. How far out are you?"

The long pause does nothing to calm my elevated heartbeat.

Finally, Rome replies. "Are you sure?"

"I'm sure Orlando needs you for more than just chauffeur duty! Of course, I'm sure. Park in the back. What can I do to set things up for him while you're on your way? Can I call a doctor?" But as soon as I say the words, I know how stupid and naïve I sound.

"Doctors in Mayfield won't give us the time of day. I can

help him; I just need a place to lie him down where we won't be attacked."

"Come to the salon. Rome, now."

His second long pause makes me want to throttle him. Orlando is the least snuggly of all the Valentinos, but I have a special place in my heart for that big lug.

I exhale only when Rome complies with a breathy, "Thanks. I'm on my way."

I don't totally know how to prepare for a stab wound, but I figure clean towels are the way to go. Luckily, I have those in spades. I grab a stack and bring them to my office, and then set about clearing a space for Orlando to lie down. The futon isn't the most stylish thing, but I knew I would need one, just in case my workaholic nature took charge and I started sleeping at this business, the same way I did when I opened my first two locations.

I tug on the couch until it's a bed. Then I cover that with towels. I pour a glass of water for Orlando, casting around for anything that might be helpful in this situation.

I wish I could tell Declan about this. He's a paramedic. He would know how to stitch Orlando up just fine. But with the alliance between our families shaky as it is, I know this isn't the moment to test those limits.

Then again, just because I ask my brother for help stitching up an old friend doesn't mean anything more than that. It doesn't mean he's made his peace with all vampires, only that he is a medical professional and someone needs his attention.

Just because the entire medical community turned their backs on vampires doesn't mean my brother won't help Orlando.

With zero certainty, I call my favorite brother, nearly ending the call twice before it connects. "Declan?"

"Hey, Coco. You won't believe the obnoxious…"

"Declan, I need you to come to the salon."

"What?" His tone immediately switches from congenial to serious. "I'm looking for my keys. What's wrong?"

"Bring your medical bag."

"Coco, what happened? Don't call me; call an ambulance! Where are your meds? Do you need extra? I'll bring some. I'm on my way."

My heart constricts with love for my brother. My best friend. The fact that he procured my meds to keep on him in case I run out is a testament to how badly we missed each other while I was away. "It's not me who needs the help, Declan. Orlando was stabbed in the West End. It's not safe for them to go to their home yet. Rome is bringing Orlando to the salon. I don't know how to treat a stab wound, so I need your help."

Declan's stunned silence comes to a crashing end when his tone turns shrill. "I don't know how to treat a vampire! Coco, why did Rome call you?"

I mean, I called him, but I know that's not the thing to say.

A new worry settles in my stomach. I called Rome because I had a hunch that something was wrong. I couldn't possibly have known or guessed this was what my gut was telling me, yet somehow, I knew to call.

How?

I shake my head at myself, shelving that concern for another, less harrowing day. "Declan, I don't know how to help Orlando, but he saved my life back in the day. I owe him this and more. Please, Declan. Bring your medical bag and help me with this."

"I mean, I..." I can hear the debate banging around in my brother's mind, so it doesn't touch his tongue. When Declan answers, there is less certainty. In fact, there is a hefty dose of wariness that I know isn't going to magically melt away on the drive over. "Okay, Coco. I'm on my way. I really don't know how to help a vampire, but I can at least give it the old college try." He snorts at his phrasing. "Of course, they don't teach any of this in college or medical school. I've never treated a vampire for anything, much less a stab wound."

"You're still miles better equipped for this than I am. Thank you, Declan."

"Of course." I can tell he is calculating the dread in my voice, because he softens back into the big brother I will never stop needing. "Hey, it's going to be okay. Vampires rarely suffer from anything other than starvation."

"Thirst," I correct him.

"You know what I mean. If the knife didn't hit his heart, he'll be fine." I can hear his car's engine starting up, and a portion of my stress fades. "Take a pill, Coco. I can hear how worked up you are." When I begin to muster a believable protest, he cuts in. "If Orlando is bad off, I'll need your hands steady so you can help me. Take a pill. That's what they're there for."

My jaw firms, but I know Declan is right. I hate it, though. I despise my bottle of pills because I never seem to stop relying on them. I want to be normal already. I've worked too hard to still have to lean on medication to get me through the day.

One day, this will be behind me. I'll run so far from the trauma that it will never catch up.

One day.

After I end the call with Declan and reluctantly pop one of my pills, I have no idea what else to do to prepare. I busy myself sterilizing a pair of scissors and then I get out the thread our aesthetician uses for threading eyebrows. I'm sure this isn't the medical grade stuff, but it's all I have, so it will have to do. My pathetic first aid kit mocks me from underneath the reception desk, but I grab it anyway.

We are going to need a lot of band-aids.

When Rome's fist pounds on the backdoor, I race to let

them in. We are still far from our ten in the morning opening time, but I glance around to make sure no one sees the bleeding vampire who is leaning heavily on Rome. I have no idea what sort of trouble they might be in, or if my father's got an alert out on them.

"Thanks for this, I..."

But there's no time for pleasantries. I drape Orlando's other arm around my shoulder and help Rome get him to my office. "Just back there. I didn't know how to set up for this, but if you tell me what you need, I can get it for you."

Rome is sweating, his expression firmer than I usually see him on our Wednesdays together at the beach. Still, he manages a modicum of softness for me, even mid-crisis. "You're perfect. Thank you, tré-sur."

I try not to focus on the sticky crimson staining Orlando's white shirt and black trousers, but it plagues my vision all the same.

Orlando will be okay. He's a vampire. A punctured lung isn't the same for him as it would be for me. Though, his breathing sounds very much irreparably impaired. Orlando's inhales are ragged, shallow and strained. I can tell it's hard for him to gather any useable oxygen without exhausting himself. On top of which, being stabbed doesn't exactly tickle.

It's hard to hold onto someone who is both heavy and slick with sweat and blood, but Rome and I manage to lower Orlando down onto my futon. I am careful with his legs as I lift them so he can lie supine. Rome busies himself tearing open Orlando's shirt. Both their faces are gaunt and pinched with pain.

When Declan knocks on the backdoor, Rome stiffens. "Whoever it is, send them away. Orlando is a screamer."

"What?" I flinch at the implications that this is about to get a lot worse before it gets better. "It's Declan. I called him."

It's the only thing that yanks Rome's focus from Orlando's still seeping wound. His nostrils flare as his wild gaze focuses in on me. "You did what?"

I tug on my fingers, anxious that I did the wrong thing. "He's a paramedic. I thought he could help."

Rome doesn't exactly raise his voice at me, but there is clear displeasure coating every syllable. "Nurses and doctors have no idea how to treat vampires. Declan is useless in this situation."

Shame washes through me that I reached out to the wrong person. Still, I move to the backdoor and let my brother in.

Declan might look like Father and Fintan, but for the unmitigated sense in his soul that divides him from the others. His rounded jaw is stern but his gait is determined as he stalks in, medical bag gripped in his right hand. "I'm ready."

Though we both know neither of us are.

11

TEARS

COLETTE

Rome's voice is clipped with barely contained disdain as he presses towels to Orlando's chest. I'm not sure there are enough towels in the world to get the bleeding to stop. "I've got this. I only bothered your sister because we were in the area. I needed a safe place to hide Orlando so I could get this under control."

This is far more blood than I am used to seeing. It keeps rippling out of Orlando in a never-ending stream of gore.

Declan sets down his bag, standing near Orlando's head but still giving the two ample space. "You made the right choice, bringing him here."

Rome grunts his non-response, which I think means the two are making peace with each other's presence.

I love Declan for many things, not the least of which is his ability to see through the clutter of a situation and hone in on the important aspects, even if they are buried beneath drama and aggression.

Declan motions to Orlando's chest. "It looks like you're trying to get the bleeding to stop. That's good. With a human, it would already be clotting, but I see this is different."

I stand with my back to the far wall, tugging on my fingers as gratitude sweeps over me. Declan is trying to educate himself. He doesn't operate from a place of bull-headed self-importance, which I know means he will go much farther than most in life.

Rome has every right to lash out. He finally has someone in the medical profession listening to him. It would be his right to unload the decades of injustice and rant about how shortsighted and biased the medical system is. They don't train their professionals to care for all people, only the ones they are most like.

I can see the rage tightening Rome's shoulders and stiffening his movements as he presses more towels to Orlando's chest, but when he speaks, Rome is remarkably measured. "Vampires take at least twice as long to clot, from what I've seen of human injuries. He will need to feed well before I get him stitched up because he's lost a lot of blood." Then he jerks his chin to the side. "Towel."

Relief floods me. Rome, the man who needs nothing and no one, is leaning on my brother. Declan is the one human who is trustworthy enough to blur the lines between what he's been taught and what he knows he will one day have to teach.

Declan grabs up a fresh towel. Instead of handing it to Rome, he scoots Rome out of the way and presses the fabric to Orlando's chest, giving my boyfriend a break. "This is how I would do it for a human. Is this right?"

Rome nods once. It's a tight, jerky motion, but they are communicating. They're not fighting over something most people won't bring up because it is so controversial.

I am a fascinated fly on the wall, watching history unfold before me.

Plus, the notion of my brother getting along with my boyfriend is a gift I will treasure for a long time.

Except in my imagination, Rome isn't as gaunt as he is now. "You're pale," I comment. "You're thirsty."

Rome shakes his head while Orlando struggles to breathe. "Orlando needs blood." He motions to his own form. "This is just adrenaline and a few cuts. I can last as long as I need to, but Orlando needs blood now. I have to go to the blood bank, but I'm afraid to leave him."

Declan shakes his head. "You can't leave us. I need you to talk me through this." I can see the dilemma playing out on my brother's face. "My blood will have to do. Which comes first, the suture or replenishing his blood? Which is top priority?"

My mouth pops open. Sure, the humans in Mayfield all donate blood once a month in exchange for a break on their property taxes, but for someone in my family to offer up their veins in a dire situation like this?

My hand moves to my heart. "I love you, Declan. You're a good man."

Orlando lets out a shuddering breath combined with a wheeze.

Declan doesn't look over his shoulder at me but manages a tight smile. "Don't tell the sheriff, alright? He's not all that keen on me being a good man."

I hate that he's right, but I love that Declan is his own man. He will do the right thing even if his own father would despise it.

Rome runs his hand over his face. "Are you sure? Because I get that it's a big deal, especially for your family. I'm not trying to disrespect your upbringing."

Declan extends his hand and Rome places another towel in his palm. "Yeah? Well, that's too bad. Because I'm all about the disrespect right now. We have to get the bleeding to stop first though, right?"

Rome's cadence is softer now. "I can do that. Do you have anything in your bag that will let you take your own blood and put it in a cup or something? I'm guessing your family will notice if you come home with fang marks."

"Right. I can draw my own blood." He motions to me. "Coco, can you help Rome?"

I'm not terribly squeamish at the sight of blood usually, but this amount is pure carnage.

I will my voice not to tremble, but a slight quaver betrays my fear as I step closer. "Of course."

Orlando's lashes are opening and shutting. Sweat is dripping off Orlando as he fights to stay lucid.

"My big sweetie pie," I coo at Orlando without meaning to. There's no help needed of me until the wound clots, so I set to dabbing the sweat off his forehead. I don't care that my brother sees me kiss the top of Orlando's head. Once upon a time, he was my friend.

And always, Orlando is my rescuer.

Orlando nuzzles closer to me, leaning into my touch with a whine that's entirely precious.

He is delirious, I can tell.

Rome jerks his head toward Orlando's midsection. "Not near his face, tré-" He catches himself, but just barely. "Colette. Away from his fangs. He's not coherent, and he's thirsty. He might lose himself and try to feed off you."

That didn't dawn on me, but it makes sense. I feel like I am abandoning my friend in his hour of need as I dutifully go where Rome points.

"Hold these towels in place. You have to push down. Don't be afraid you'll crack a rib. Our bones are stronger." Rome scoots out of the way but doesn't remove his hands until mine are in place. His finger brushes against mine, announcing our scandal in front of my brother, who is right behind us.

I should relish the touch, but fear shoots through me.

"You're icy, Rome. This isn't just adrenaline. Are you hurt, too?"

A muscle in his jaw ticks. "I'm fine. Orlando needs our attention, not me."

I know Rome well enough by now to spot the lie.

Before I can argue, his nostrils flare. "Oh, that's strong. Declan, you... I..." Rome steps away, slapping his own cheeks as he backs into the far corner and sinks to the floor.

"Rome?" My fretting is useless because I cannot leave Orlando. I press down with all my weight, praying with everything in me that his wound clots enough for Declan to stitch him up. "Rome, what's wrong?"

Rome's knees are bent as he hugs his middle, looking suddenly like a little boy woken from a bad dream he's not convinced isn't real. "I'm not used to smelling fresh human blood straight out of the veins. Or if I have smelled it, I haven't been this thirsty. It's okay, Colette. Keep putting pressure on the wound." He shoves his knuckle between his teeth, holding himself back with obvious effort.

Declan swears. "How much does Orlando need?"

"As much as you can spare. Colette, lift the towel. Is the blood slowing down?"

I comply, grimacing and fighting back vomit as I inspect the wound I am ill-equipped to treat. I have never seen a stab wound through someone's chest before. It's not a thin, two-inch puncture. "This isn't one cut, Declan. It's at least... I can't tell. Maybe they cut and then dragged the knife or something. It's not a clean slice. It's all jagged and gross." I recall Rome's reason for having me look at the macabre sight. "But it's not bleeding as much right now. It's starting to clot."

Declan's voice is unsteady, but I trust his direction all the same. "Good. Now grab a clean towel and dab around the area so the ends aren't so slippery. Rome, how does she disinfect the area?"

"No need. We aren't prone to infection. You need to suture him now. I can't do it," Rome admits. I can hear the self-loathing in his voice. "My fingers are rigid from thirst, so you'll have to do it, Declan."

"Not a problem. Let me finish this up. There." Declan sets his cup of blood on the floor and then stands, but he wobbles on his feet. "Whoa."

I let out a high-pitched whimper, but luckily, my brother catches himself before he falls. Declan sags against the wall and then lowers himself to his knees. "I'm going to need a minute."

I whine in Rome's direction.

Before he opens his mouth, I know what he is going to say.

Rome manages a wan smile for me. "I'll talk you through it."

Thank goodness I took my pill already.

Declan's heavy breathing doesn't reassure me one bit.

Rome's voice is pinched but feigning calm as best he can. "Reach inside the tear and find where his lung was punctured. When you find the rip, pinch it shut with your finger and your thumb and stitch with the other hand."

Declan is barely upright. "Huh. That's not how humans do it."

"Are you serious?" But even as I voice my concern, my hands begin to obey.

Years ago, Orlando fought his way through men with guns and ammo that was potentially laced with my deadly blood. He saved me when I was fifteen years old.

Now it's time to pay back that favor.

12

BLOOD, TEARS AND VOMIT
COLETTE

Vomit rises in my throat as I reach for the thread that I procured earlier, which is most certainly the wrong type.

"My bag," Declan reminds me.

Thank goodness. I fish around in my brother's medic bag until I find a sealed pack that looks like the needle and thread I will be needing.

Because I am going to have to...

No. I can't think about it yet. Not until the moment I absolutely have to.

After I tear open the package, I manage to thread the needle after two misses.

Rome is breathing through his teeth as he crawls slowly across my floor, his movements rigid. I screech my horror when I notice a trail of clearly fresh blood streaking across the wood behind him. "You're injured, you stubborn ass! I knew you were hurt!"

Rome doesn't look up, but keeps his gaze focused on the cup beside my brother on the floor. "It's just a scratch." Then to my brother, he says, "Orlando needs that blood, Declan."

"If I pick it up, I'm going to drop it," Declan admits.

Rome swears and then tips the cup to his lips. "Just a sip, so I can get it to him."

I whirl around the second Rome finishes his gulp. "I can do it. You sit down and think about how ridiculous your pride is. Sit right there and don't move. I can barely stand to look at you; I'm so mad."

Rome chuckles, which I'll admit, isn't a sound I expected I might hear in this dire situation. "Worry about Orlando. Stitch his lung shut first. Once he can breathe, then feed him some blood. After that, sew up the surface wound."

I'm struggling to put his directions in order, so great is my fear that I will be the cause of Orlando's death because I am lousy with a needle and thread. The scream that ekes out behind closed lips announces my terror to the room as I reach into Orlando's open chest. I try not to vomit into his chest cavity as I fish around for the hole in his lung.

Orlando's eyelids open in terror mixed with agony, no doubt not loving the sensation of a finger massaging his vital organ. He gasps for breath, gripping my free arm as best he can with slippery and rigid fingers. He wheezes while he tries to work out a protest.

"I'm sorry, I'm sorry, I'm sorry," I ramble as I poke around for far too long. Tears cloud my vision, but that's the least of my worries. I cannot find the tear because everything is slimy and scary, and I have zero medical training for such things.

Tears slip down my cheeks and splash into Orlando's open wound, making the whole thing even more sloppy and chaotic.

I don't know what I'm doing. I am inches away from barfing my morning tea all over him, which I'm guessing isn't something a person prefers.

Rome is trying to talk me through it, but I can't hear him over my sobbing, which has now become audible. I bite down on my lower lip, knowing I am the only person in this room who can deal with this situation, however clumsily.

My fingers find new purpose as I stare into Orlando's eyes, marking his silent scream as the moment I promise him I will not fail.

Touching Orlando's lung is close to what I imagine running my finger over a giant, slimy eyeball might feel like. I take my time, searching for the smallest nick that might be causing the problem.

Orlando grips my forearm as much as he is able, shaking and shuddering as he wheezes.

Only I realize the wheezing sound doesn't stop once he has taken in a breath.

I angle my head down, crying still as I listen to his lung, locating the sound of a faint hissing nearer to his sternum than I was touching. My finger glides toward the center, skidding across a slit that can't be more than half an inch long. "I found it!" I shout, sobbing as I pinch the hole shut. My fingers are slick with Orlando's blood, but they pinch with purpose.

Finally, Orlando's lung expands the way it should. I am motivated by the urge to keep him alive, of course, but also, I know that the sooner I stitch up the tear on his lung, the sooner I can get my hand out of him and go vomit in the toilet.

A memory pops into my mind, thankfully distracting me from the gore. "Do you remember when you helped me cheat at Go Fish?" I am not sure Orlando is coherent enough to hear me. Perhaps I am revisiting this memory for my own sanity's sake.

Either way, the story spills out of me as more tears surface.

"I kept losing, and I didn't understand how. I didn't realize that the guys were holding back their cards from me, even though I would ask for what I knew they had." I sniffle through my recollection as my fingers work unsteadily. "I got frustrated and was about to cry, so you pulled me onto your lap and helped me learn how to cheat at cards. You whispered in my ear the right things to say. I learned how to play dirty that day."

I still my stitching as a sob escapes me, compromising my vision. "I loved you for it. I still do."

I shake my head as a hysterical one-noted laugh belts out of me. "I should be thinking about all the times you let me ride on your shoulders, or when you gave me half your ice cream when mine fell off my cone. I should be remembering the sweetness." I sniffle as my mind begins to refocus. "I love you exactly as you are, Orlando. You're my big sweetie pie." My lower lip trembles. "You can't leave me. You can't. Not when the world is still cheating, and I don't always know how to play dirty. I need you."

Rome's voice steadies my anxiety as much as mere words are able. "He will live, Colette. Orlando will never leave us when we still need him this badly."

I nod, taking in a deep breath so I can finish the job before me.

It's not the prettiest of stitching, but the muscle holds after I do two rows, making sure there are no gaps. Best of all, I can't hear any more wheezing or hissing.

More of my tears fall into Orlando's open chest cavity, lubricating his lung.

I don't even realize Rome is at Orlando's side near his head until he speaks, splitting my singular focus. "You did it. That's perfect, Colette. He needs to drink now before you sew up the flesh wound." Rome tilts Orlando up just enough so the man doesn't choke when he sips from the mug of blood, which usually holds my morning tea.

"I can do the rest," my brother says from behind me. Declan's voice isn't exactly steady, but aside from his pallor, he looks sturdier than I feel.

I step away after handing Declan the needle and thread. I am grateful to be done contributing for the moment.

But the second Rome finishes feeding Orlando the blood, I point a slick and crimson finger in his direction. "Okay, now it's your turn. Sit down and show me what's hurting."

Rome waves off my concern, his movements still stiff. "I'm alright. It'll heal."

Though tears still streak my face, I am no less ferocious. Misplaced anger rises up in me, tightening the tenor of my tone. "Sit down right now and show me!" I thunder. "Declan is dealing with Orlando, so you're not taking help away from your cousin. Show me, Rome, or I swear, I'll give you a fresh wound to cry about!"

Rome raises his hands in surrender with a wry chuckle. "Okay, okay. It's not that big of a deal. I got caught by a bullet in the fight, but it passed through my calf, so it's fine. It really will heal on its own."

His bravery kindles my fury. "You are going to sit down right now and let me stitch it up, or so help me, Rome."

"It would make you feel better to sew me up?"

I shoot him a snotty look, my tone dripping with sarcasm. "It would be my cotton candy dream come true. Now sit down and stop pissing me off."

Rome laughs at my bratty demeanor. "Your bedside manner needs work, tré-" But he catches himself again before accidentally announcing to my brother that I am his treasure. "Colette."

He sits down in my guest chair near my desk while I grab a second needle and thread. He takes his time rolling up his pant leg. When he exposes the wound to the air, I can see why.

He flinches at my scandalized gasp. "See? Not that big a deal."

My words come out in a low seethe. "Would a big deal be your leg falling clean off? What constitutes a big deal to you?" My tears fall onto his wound as I kneel between Rome's spread knees, examining the gash as if I know what I am doing.

First I cried into Orlando's open chest, and now my tears are seeping into Rome's bullet wound.

I am frightened, which of course I cover over with anger.

I scowl up at Rome through his amused chuckle. "What am I supposed to do with this? Does it need cleaning, or do I just start sewing?"

"Is it clotted?"

"No."

"Then I'm pretty sure we're going to need another towel."

I stomp over to the depleting pile of towels and snatch one up, grimacing at the macabre job Declan has to deal with.

I am slightly less antagonized as I kneel back down between Rome's knees, putting more pressure than I would for a human wound on the back of his calf.

I don't like the sight of Rome all torn up. Even worse is that he considers a gunshot wound something that can wait. Though the sips of Declan's blood seem to have done him some good, it is clear he should be lying down.

I can feel Rome's eyes on me while I wait for his wound to clot. I want to shake him. I want to hug him. I want to kiss him. I also want to run far, far away from all of this.

But I moved back to Mayfield of my own accord, so I cannot waste my wishes, hoping for a life far from this violence.

After a minute or two, Rome's leg is finally ready for me to get to work on it. I cannot bring myself to look up at him, not even for a longing glance. If I do, I will break down all over again. This is not the time for that. I have to muscle through this and shake off my fear, pretending it's all no big deal.

If I don't, my boyfriend will have a gaping gunshot wound and no one to help him.

I bite down on my lower lip to keep it from trembling.

Every stitch is questioned and doubled to make sure he can walk without fear of tearing it all open. The tear is on the inside section of his calf, just below the sexy muscle I lust after each time I get to see him in those delicious swim trunks.

His body is precious to me.

Whoever did this has earned my vengeance.

I am careful as I sew Rome's leg, brushing my fingers over his shin to soothe his angst while I further connect my heart to his.

"Who did this?" I ask in a manner I try to keep nonchalant.

It's a bad act. Rome sees right through it. "The Easter Bunny."

"I want a name," I argue above Orlando's whimpering that quickly mutates into a howl.

Rome leans forward and tucks his stiff finger under my chin. He lifts my head so I am looking straight into his stunningly ice blue eyes.

It's not until then that I realize I've started crying all over again. My tears slip over my cheeks, but I refuse to give in to a sob.

Rome's gaze is simultaneously stern and compassionate. "I don't want you anywhere near this mess, Colette. I will handle the people who hurt my men."

My lower lip quivers, and finally a muffled sob sneaks past my lips. "You are precious to me," I whisper, dancing on the edge of danger, admitting something so obvious with my brother right behind me.

Rome touches his chest, letting me know he feels the same way. "It will be okay," he promises. "Don't I always look after the people who are important to me?"

I nod, and then refocus on the rip in his skin once he sits back, his movements stiff.

It's an effort to finish up. Everything is so slick. The curly black hair on his leg is matted and keeps getting in the way. Still, I manage to tie the knot after the last stitch, and then fold his pant leg down before I stand.

Thank goodness I didn't have to dig out a bullet. I might have vomited in his lap.

My legs are heavy and clumsy as I move toward the door. Before I open it, Declan stops me. "Coco, are you alright?"

I know what he's really asking. "I'm fine."

And it's true. My medicine kicked in before my anxiety ramped up the parts of my brain that prove problematic in a crisis.

"Come here. Show me your hands."

Declan doesn't want to see the blood; he is checking to make sure my tremors aren't acting up. Though I really don't like this kind of talk around the Valentinos (or anyone), I comply, knowing Declan will only drop it when he sees the proof. I move to his side, glancing at Orlando's chest to find it more than halfway stitched up.

Orlando passed out, but he is breathing.

I hold my hands level to the floor, noting the stillness even though I am thoroughly shaken. "See? No trouble at all."

"Good."

I jerk my thumb over my shoulder. "Now, if you'll excuse me, I'm going to go vomit in the bathroom."

Declan keeps his eyes on his job. "Happy puking, Sis."

I stumble out the door, ignoring Rome when he tells me to slow down. With every step, I can feel the bile rising, begging for release. I barely have the wherewithal to close the door behind me before I drop to my knees and hover over the bowl. This was not the morning I had planned, and the workday hasn't even started yet.

True to my prediction, my stomach needs only the barest permission to empty itself as images of Orlando's exposed lung race to the forefront of my cruel imagination. I am grateful my hair is already in a bun atop my head, so no chunks land in my tresses.

When the bathroom door opens, I barely have time to choke out a protest before more vomit pours out of me. "Go away," I moan, wishing Rome wasn't a gentleman who followed me to make sure I was okay.

"Tré-sur," he coos, dropping to his knees beside me. His palm finds my back, rubbing soothing circles while I heave into the toilet. "Breathe through it. You were amazing."

"I was terrified!" I choke out, my chest heaving while my head hovers over the bowl. "I don't know how to sew up a lung! I cried into the wound, Rome! Both your wounds! That can't be hygienic."

"Shh," he urges, soothing me while I sob into the bowl. "You were brilliant. More than that, you were brave. I don't know anyone who would have helped us the way you and Declan did today."

We both quiet while we wait for my stomach to settle. I love the feel of his hand on my back. He was shot, yet he is comforting me.

When I am convinced I've thrown up the last of everything in my stomach, I flush the toilet and try to stand.

"No, no. Let me help you. Do you need water?" He supports my weak body and leads me to the sink. He turns on the water and cups his hands, bringing the shallow well to my lips.

I'm so gross. I'm covered in blood and I just threw up. Still, he looks at me as if I am the most beautiful creature he has ever seen. I sip from his hands, scared and mired in a wish that all of this could somehow be better than the nightmare it is.

Rome takes his time warming up the flow so he can wash my hands and my arms. His touch is stiff but tender as he takes his time with each inch made available to him. I love the way he tends to me when I am completely lost and mired in angst.

He doesn't stop at my arms, but laves water over my cheeks and neck, rinsing away the blood, bile and tears.

"I'm gross," I protest, but I don't pull away. "And I yelled at you."

Rome sniggers. "You sure did. I loved every second of it."

I scowl up at him. "You lied. You said you weren't hurt."

"I'm not. See? Some angel came down from the heavens and made it all better."

My lower lip quivers all over again. The second he's wiped away the blood and tears from my face, my eyes well up once more. "You scared me!"

Rome softens, tilting his head to the side. He should be sitting down. He's gaunt and leaning his hip heavily on the edge of the sink, but he's still here, looking after me. "I'm sorry, little cannoli. Everything's okay now, though."

I scoff my disbelief. "Is it? Because I don't see how. There are so many things wrong with this situation. I should have been able to take you to a hospital! Declan should have been trained to help vampires. I've been all proud of myself for helping get the parks cleaned up, but it's a tiny patch on a gaping wound that might never heal!" My breath comes in stuttering fits and spurts. "All of this is messed up, and the best I can do is cry all over Orlando's body while he tries to breathe! Who did this?"

Rome shushes me gently and pulls me into his arms. "The system has been broken for a long time. You're despairing, but this is the first day I have true hope that it might not always be this way. Declan helped us. He gave his blood and learned how to sew up a vampire. It's a big win for my kind, Coletta."

It's pathetic, seeing an inch of forced progress and feeling elation, but I don't have the heart to take that away from him. "Can I still be mad about the whole thing?"

"Of course, my dear. Be as angry as you like, only do it while you're in my arms." He sighs contentedly when I rest my head on his shoulder, burying my tears in his shirt for safe keeping. "It's okay," he promises, even though we both know I don't believe him. "It's all going to be okay."

The steadiness in his voice comes out like a command issued to the universe, telling it firmly that it has carried on long enough, upsetting me as it has. He kisses my hair, his strong arms caging me in. Now I have a steady fortress to weather this storm, though the raging wind might never truly go away in our lifetimes.

Still, I cling to Rome, holding him as tight as he holds onto me. "I'm scared," I admit in a whisper I trust will stay between us.

"Then I won't let go until that fear gets quieter."

It's a beautiful promise, and one I take him up on. Rome holds me until my last tear runs dry, buried in the fabric of his shirt over his heart.

I will never stop adoring this man, no matter how slow the world turns toward a new horizon.

13

APART IN THE PARK
COLETTE

I do not want to be at any park today, much less cleaning it up. I want to be at Orlando's bedside, holding his hand while he heals.

"It's okay," Rome reminds me. "Vampires heal faster than humans. Orlando is already breathing without issue. A few more days, and he'll be running marathons."

I glare at Rome while I pick up a glass bottle and throw it in the garbage. "I sincerely hope you know me better than to pacify me with a joke. I shouldn't be here. I should be with Orlando."

Rome keeps his voice quiet. "You know it would be a bad idea for you to be in our house. The world is still wary of you being around vampires. It's not like it was when you were a little girl." He motions around Friendly Park. "Vampires like you where they can see you when you're in the

West End. The park is fine. Inside my home, unfortunately, is not."

My lips purse at the injustice. "But Orlando is my friend! What if he needs a glass of water but it's too far away?"

"Nico is with him."

I shove a crusty flyer into the trash bag. "Oh, that's reassuring. If I ever fall ill, I will never forgive you if you put Nico in charge of my care."

Rome chuckles, though I don't see what's funny about it. "Duly noted."

He is limping. Rome shouldn't be here. He was shot two nights ago. He should be lying down with his feet up. I'm no doctor, but I can't imagine it's healthy or safe to be walking on a leg that was just sewn up two nights ago.

But as I've already told him this three times so far today and he has ignored me every time, I suppose there's no use in telling him a fourth time that we've got this, and he should go home.

Though, Rome being here is keeping me from murdering my eldest brother, which I guess is a bonus.

I brush a leaf off my jeans. "Fintan, will you stop 'supervising' and actually be useful? Leaning on a rusty poll isn't the same as digging the thing out. It needs to be removed so a new one can be put in."

I can barely stand to look at Fintan. Knowing he has been selling me to men for twenty thousand dollars per blind date is a betrayal of which I did not think him capable. I haven't confronted him yet, but the anger boils in my blood all the same.

My eldest brother's thin upper lip curls in my direction. "You got me to come out here. I picked up a few pieces of garbage. Best let the vampire trash handle their own trash."

The reporters have gone home for the day, leaving me with my brothers, Declan's friend, my father, Rome, half a dozen vampires and four policemen. None of them stops me when I throw down my black plastic bag and march with purpose toward my oldest brother. "Fintan Kennedy, you are without a doubt the most spoiled boy I have ever met. You don't get the photo op if you're not working. Grab that shovel and dig out the swing set poll. It's rusted through, so it has to go."

Fintan plants his feet more firmly where he stands, doing nothing but getting on my nerves. "I'm taking a break."

"A break from what? You've been standing there being completely useless for the last half an hour."

The sheriff wipes the sweat off his brow. "She's not wrong, Fintan. Either help or go home."

I can't believe my father is taking my side. That hardly ever happens. He and Fintan are thick as thieves.

I have Declan and Fintan has Father. That's how it works.

I can tell Declan is surprised, too. He straightens and catches my eye, offering a hapless shrug because it is just as strange to him as it is to me whenever Father is nice to me. Or him. Or anyone, really.

Fintan takes the shovel with a dramatic eye roll and starts digging around the post like a novice. It is clear he hasn't done anything with his hands in a while.

Or perhaps Fintan is just being a petulant brat, which wouldn't surprise me one bit.

Fintan's griping is loud. "I don't know why I have to be here. I was out late playing poker at my buddy's warehouse in Dazier. I barely slept."

I roll my eyes. "You drove an hour away for a poker game? I hope you won big."

By the way Fintan is stabbing at the dirt with a sneer on his face, I can tell that is not the case.

My eldest brother's grousing is annoying. "I shouldn't have to be here. I didn't let my end of the city fall to crap. Rome is barely moving over there."

My volume rises to match my brother's. "Rome was shot, you idiot! What's your excuse? Are you missing each of your arm muscles? Is that why shoveling is such a chore for you?"

Declan starts singing, like he always does when Fintan and I go at each other. It's his way of coping, so I know I have to tone it down and get my temper under control. I don't care if I stress out Fintan, who doesn't care about anyone but himself. But I don't want any part of anything that makes Declan upset.

I turn toward him, my shoulders lowering. "Sorry, Declan. I'll stop."

Rome watches our exchange from the periphery, taking in the varying relational health between me and my brothers.

The sheriff is sweating, even though it is a little nippy out. He motions for one of his officers to come over and help him yank the support for the seesaw out of the ground, now that he is finished digging around it.

Declan follows my gaze and, knowing that the sheriff doesn't like or listen to me, he offers our father a bottle of water. "Sit on down, Sheriff. Let me help the guys."

My father takes the water and sits down on the park bench that was repainted yesterday. It's one of the few things that didn't need to be yanked out of the ground and replaced completely.

"Your family is fun to watch," Rome comments when he drops trash in my garbage bag, limping as he comes. "I thought us Valentinos were dysfunctional, but I think you might rival us."

"Challenge accepted. It's Fintan who's the problem. And the sheriff, usually. Declan and I are the good ones."

Rome chuckles at me while keeping his distance. "I have no doubt. Then again, both the sheriff and Fintan are here, helping the community. That's got to count in their favor at least a little."

"Yeah, yeah. I guess every now and then Hell freezes over. And let's call a spade a spade; Fintan only helps when I make him."

"He's got his reasons to hate us. The fact that he's here at all is a big step."

I glare at Rome, though my venom is meant for Fintan. "You deserve more than table scraps of kindness, Rome. You all do."

He leans on the side of the slide, his gait wobbly. I know he's in pain, but he doesn't want to admit it. Especially not after Fintan's comment about this being Rome's responsibility and not everyone's shared burden.

I put down the garbage bag and take off my gloves. "Easy. Let's get you to the bench. You can sit with the sheriff and check him for aliens controlling his brain to make him nicer."

Rome shakes his head. "I'm fine. My leg is a little tender, is all."

"Of course it's tender; you were shot." My voice catches as the image of him bleeding and me sewing him up in my salon resurfaces in my mind. I've been trying to block that out for two nights now to no avail. I don't like to picture my boyfriend bleeding, and I don't like thinking that anyone would hate him enough to shoot him.

Don't they know that he makes raspberry cannoli by hand?

Don't they know he reads poetry to his girlfriend over the phone?

Don't they understand that he is the only optimist left in the West End?

The world needs him.

I need him.

I study Rome's lax stance as he grips the side of the slide.

Don't they see what a treasure he is?

I take a chance and slip his arm around my shoulder, guessing that no one would think anything fishy is going on if I'm just helping a friend to the bench. That's not weird.

But we only make it three steps before Declan's voice turns sharp. "Coco, don't do that."

My cheeks heat. I step away as if I've been caught undressing Rome in public. "I was just helping him to the bench, Declan. He really shouldn't be standing this much on his leg."

Declan trots over to Rome, his friend trailing behind. "I can help him. You're going to make him uncomfortable, being so near him." Declan ruffles my hair with a firmness to his smile. "I've got him, Youngblood."

Oh, right. I'm not supposed to be this close to vampires for their own safety.

I'm guessing gnawing on Rome's lower lip isn't exactly safe, either.

I watch forlornly as Declan and his buddy help Rome to the bench, where he sits down beside my father.

I hate that I don't get to help him, that I have to watch someone else help my own boyfriend when he needs it.

I know this is part of the gig. We are different and the world might never be ready for us. But having to distance myself from Rome when he is clearly in pain isn't how I want to live my life.

But because Rome is worth enduring the sadness of being socially distanced from the love of my life, I watch from across the playground as my brother chats casually with my boyfriend.

I swallow hard as I pick up the trash bag and continue my work.

This isn't how I was expecting to find someone worth dating, yet here I am, staring at the man I want to help, but standing back because we can never be together in public.

14

FAMILY DINNER
COLETTE

Family dinners weren't a thing growing up. But after my father insisted upon having one weeks ago that never came to fruition, we knew we couldn't put it off any longer.

It's actually not as bad as I thought it would be. It's kind of entertaining, watching Declan and Fintan argue over who got the bigger pork chop, while my father ignores them both and takes double the mashed potatoes. Everything is simpler at the dinner table, since the food distracts us from our major personality clashes. My father isn't the authoritative bulldog he always has to be, and my brothers have turned into adolescents who giggle at fart jokes.

I didn't know my father could cook.

Or that he liked having us in his house.

Per his strict instructions, there is no work talk, and no

politics. It's just the Kennedy four at our finest and most juvenile.

It's been two weeks since Orlando and Rome were sewn up in my salon. Orlando sends me over a delivery of a decaf cinnamon vanilla latte every day from the coffee shop across the street. My big sweetie pie is back on his feet and back at Rome's side, which seems like the most ridiculously short recovery time ever, but Rome assured Declan and me that it was normal.

Declan has mired himself deeper into the scandal to which I introduced to him. He's met up with the two vampires several times in the past two weeks, asking question after question and taking notes on how to treat different vampiric maladies.

I love Declan.

Best of all, I haven't had to take my medication in three days. I know I need to talk to my doctor before weaning myself off, but technically, that's not what I'm trying to do. I am just taking them less often, is all. The salon is coming along smashingly, and every night, Rome reads me to sleep.

He's my good medicine now.

So I don't need my pills as often.

Fintan grins at Declan and me. Though a smile is nothing to be wary of, Fintan is known for having several ulterior motives up his sleeve, so I never get too attached to his moments of elation. He piles on more brussels sprouts while I butter another roll. "Everyone have seconds. If there are leftovers, Dad will make less next time. No one beg off of seconds tonight. I want just as much of this food next time, so you two had better clear your plates."

I was full ten minutes ago, but I know there's no arguing with Fintan when food is on the line. I dutifully take more salad but pass on the sprouts. "I'm so full, Fintan. I didn't eat like this in Lonmure."

"You never ate so good." Declan elbows me. "Eat up. You're wasting away. All that manual labor at the park means we need to keep up with our calorie intake."

Not to be the stereotypical waif, but I simply cannot keep up with the appetites of three grown men. And more manual labor only makes me want to take a nap, not eat my weight in mashed potatoes.

I'm so glad all the parks in the West End are finally updated. It took hardly any time at all, what with so many volunteers pitching in.

Once the food is consumed and the table cleared by Declan and myself, Fintan breaks out the cards so we can play poker over dessert.

Declan starts acting out the best scenes of Blood Ninja Disco VII, complete with karate chop action after he shoves the final plate into the dishwasher.

Fintan motions to me. "I'm glad you two have each other. I had to take him to the last one that came out. That was a long night." Fintan's phone rings, but when he checks the caller ID, he frowns. "Gotta take this outside."

The loan sharking business never sleeps. One would think Fintan would be satisfied with owning a restaurant, but apparently he needs his hands in multiple pots. He can take calls from the restaurant in front of us, no problem, but when he has to take a call outside, I know it's his side hustle.

Emphasis on the "hustle".

While I haven't forgiven Fintan or confronted him about the fact that he has been selling dates with me to random strangers, he hasn't been all that insufferable tonight, so I don't mind staying late for dessert and a game of poker.

"Be quick," the sheriff warns his eldest son.

Fintan nods and steps out the front door while Declan entertains our father with the best and worst of the dance numbers. To be fair, Father never approves of anything, so the fact that he doesn't take a shine to our favorite movie franchise is no real surprise.

"One day, you have to watch them with us." Declan swipes the beginnings of sweat off his forehead and plops down in his seat at the table. He is slightly thicker around the middle than the wiry Fintan, but that doesn't slow down his dance moves.

"Which one?" the sheriff asks, which, I'll admit is more interest than he has ever shown in anything Declan says.

"All of them," Declan replies without missing a beat. "Start to finish. It's the only way to appreciate the whole story arc they're going for."

It's the most the sheriff has ever pretended to care about something so silly and meaningless. He doesn't like fun. And I cannot picture him sitting through a movie that's thirty percent dancing.

When Fintan comes back inside, his short light brown hair is wet from the rain I hear starting up outside. His expression is grim and his gait stilted. He throws his phone down on the table and points to the picture that's still lit up. "Care to explain this?" he all but growls at me.

My brows furrow. "What?" I lean in and take a look, my lips pursing when I make out a snapshot of a piece of paper with a clear threat typed across it.

"THE REVOLUTION WILL NOT BE STOPPED. IF YOU WON'T GIVE US your blood, we'll take it by force. We will not stop until the leeches of the world are stamped out."

15

THE SHERIFF'S LITTLE GIRL
COLETTE

I can feel three sets of eyes on me, but my gaze doesn't move from the picture on Fintan's phone. "Where did you get this?"

Fintan snarls at me. "That's not the question, Coco. Why didn't you tell us you were getting threats again?"

Finally, my chin lifts so I can focus on my oldest brother's anger. "This is the first I'm seeing this. Where did you get it?"

Fintan scoffs, all sense of our earlier levity gone. "I know you, Coco. I know when you're hiding information. You don't want to come clean because you don't want us to send you overseas again." His palm slaps down on the tabletop. "Your life is more important than this city! Don't you get that? I'm not going to let them take you out, like they did Liz."

It's a sore subject, and not one any of us bring up

unless clear duress is involved. Fintan's girlfriend being drained by a vampire nearly a decade ago isn't a wound any of us will ever forget—least of all Fintan. That wound is never going to stop bleeding.

I don't remember much about Liz. It was so long ago. But I do recall their constant need to break up and get back together over and over again. The fact that she died the night after one of their big fights?

I'm not sure who Fintan hates more—vampires or himself.

"Where did you find this?" I ask again, though Fintan is pacing now, so I know he's not listening. He looks like the sheriff now more than ever.

Though at the moment, my father just looks tired.

Fintan moves back and forth across the dining room floor, gesturing with his arms. "We told you it was dangerous for you to come home. A salon opened any other place would be just fine. But you know you're plopping yourself smack in the middle of a bad situation, coming back here. The rebel factions still exist, no matter how much we all want to believe they came to their senses." His thin lips firm in my direction. "You need to go back to Lonmure."

Everything in me steels against this logic that's been shoved down my throat for years. My upper lip curls at my brother. "I won't be bullied out of my home. Not by you and not by this letter. Whoever sent this is a coward. I belong wherever I put myself, which is exactly here. Peace is possible, and I am not leaving until it comes to Mayfield."

Declan remains beside me, scooping up my hand in solidarity. "Any clue who sent it?"

Fintan shakes his head.

Our father's low voice hasn't said much, but finally, he puts volume to the question I have asked three times. "Where did you find this, Fintan?"

Sure, when I say it, it goes ignored, but when the sheriff says it, all of a sudden Fintan has perfect hearing.

Fintan turns his head away. "One of my men was paying a visit to a loan that's past due. Fairfax—the guy who owns the warehouse where we play poker." When the name doesn't rouse familiarity in me, Fintan continues. "Fairfax walked by the salon and found it taped to the front door of Colette's store."

Lying. Fintan is lying. He always angles his chin away from whomever he's speaking to when he reaches past the truth for something less noble. I have never pointed out his obvious tell because I like knowing when I am being lied to.

If this Fairfax person didn't find the note taped to the door of my salon, then where did he find it? And why is Fintan lying about that detail?

My father slips out of his newly acquired family night dad-mode with ease. He fits into his sheriff persona far more naturally. "Send that to me. I'll need the original, of course. Did your man touch it?"

"No. It's still taped there. He's not an idiot."

"Good. I'll take it from here." Daddy points to me. "Any other threats, Coco?"

I hold up my hands. "No. Not that I've seen. I didn't lock up tonight, so it's possible it was there and I didn't see it because I left early to come here."

"Okay, then. You're staying here tonight."

I stand, unwilling to play this game. "No. I appreciate it, but I'm not going down this road again. My life is my own. I'm not going to move overseas or live at my daddy's house because someone is trying to scare me."

Fintan's volume makes me cringe. "They're not trying to scare you; they're trying to steal you and weaponize you! Tell me you get that!"

I refuse to be frightened in front of my brothers and my father. I make a point of keeping my voice level. "I get that just fine, Fintan. That's why I am going to my house. That was part of the deal. I come back to the city, and I get to live on my own. You agreed, provided you got to auction me off to the most eligible men in the city. I have a home all my own now, so that's where I'll be."

Declan squeezes my hand. "How about I follow you home. It's on my way."

Fintan's authoritarian demeanor brings out the bull in me. But Declan's genuine worry softens the steadfast upward tilt of my chin. "Fine. But we're not giving in to this threat, understood? That's all this is."

I can tell Fintan's got plenty to say on the subject, but the sheriff cuts him off. "You leave it to me, kids. Coco, I wouldn't have let you come home if I didn't believe you'd be safe. I'll get to the bottom of who's threatening my little girl."

His little girl?

The sheriff never talks like that, so I know he's worked up. My father being affectionate is a sure sign that things are worse than I am aware.

Or it's a sign that my father has had a stroke and thinks I am someone else. Someone he cares about.

Worry begins to seep into my pores, but I can't let it turn me into a closet case. I won't do that again. I've worked too hard to become a stable person who doesn't jump at shadows.

We don't play poker tonight. No one is in the mood for games. The sheriff is already making calls when Declan pulls me from the table and helps me thread my arms through my coat. I can hear the rain outside, but it's not storming yet. Still, I can feel one brewing.

"You sure you don't want to stay here tonight?" Declan asks me, this time making sure to keep the question between us, so it's not a challenge I have to fend off.

"No," I decide. "I didn't come home so I could live in fear. My house is perfectly safe. If someone was going to abduct me, they would have. This is a note. Threats are the tools of cowards. I am not afraid of a coward."

Declan doesn't argue, but he sticks close as we walk together through the curtain of rain to our respective vehicles. He can spot my tremors better than most, so I do my best to keep my movements shrouded in shadow as much as possible.

A storm is on the horizon—another reason to hurry home.

After I lock myself in my car, I want to shake my fist at my entire family, but my wrist is twitching too violently for such gestures.

It's happening again. The racist scum want to eradicate the tax-paying vampires of the world, and they want to use me to do it.

I will not be used. Not again.

"I'm safe," I say aloud to no one but myself. "I'm not going to be abducted again."

My stomach churns as my nerves peak. The horrific memories I try never to think about confront me over and over, reminding me that yes, there are some very sick men in the world.

I don't want to break down, but the stress that comes from surviving three separate abductions isn't something I would wish on my worst enemy. My fingers are shaking so badly; I worry that attempting the ten-minute drive from my father's house to my home might be a poor decision.

A minute into the drive, my phone rings through the interior of my car. "I'm fine!" I say in lieu of a greeting when I answer the call over Bluetooth. Fintan is never going to let this go. "The note changes nothing, Fintan. I am not moving overseas again."

"What note?" Rome asks, his low voice sending my already taxed nerves into overdrive. "Why would you be moving out of the city?"

16

I AM NORMAL
COLETTE

I swallow hard, rotating my twitching left wrist as I drive with my right hand. "Sorry," I say to Rome, hoping to avoid talking about this terrible evening to my boyfriend. "I thought you were Fintan. Never mind. How are you?" My voice is mechanically pleasant now.

"What note?" Rome repeats.

My fingers are trembling as I explain as succinctly as possible the threatening note Fintan's buddy found taped to the front door of my salon. "It's fine. That sort of thing will always happen."

"Where are you?"

"Driving home from my father's house. Declan's following me to make sure I get in safe. I've got a decent security system. There's nothing to worry about."

Though, as I say this, my fingers shake so badly, I worry I shouldn't be behind the steering wheel at all.

I only just got my license back last year. Testing the limits of my condition was a bad idea. I shouldn't have tried to take myself off my medication. Or perhaps I should have tried a method other than going cold turkey.

To be fair, I packed my purse for a family dinner, not trauma central. My pills are at home. I didn't think I would need them at my father's house.

I've been doing so well. Even with the addition of manual labor working at the parks, I've been able to wean myself off the pills well enough.

Well, it was good while it lasted.

Stupid Fintan, yelling at me about that stupid note.

Rome's reply is the perfect thing I didn't know I needed to hear. "How can I help?" It's not a swooping need to control. He's not telling me what to do. He's letting me call the shots and offering support.

I let out a shaky breath. "There's nothing to be done. My father and Fintan are looking into the letter. They seemed pretty upset about it. The sheriff usually digs until he hits the bottom when he's amped up about something."

"Where are you now? Can I meet you somewhere?"

"I'm in the East End. Almost home. Everyone's overreacting. It's all fine. I have everything under control." Though, I realize when my words come out, they are coated in obvious denial.

My hands are practically jumping now, with muscles malfunctioning up my arms. I swear aloud. I knew this was going to happen. I just hoped I could make it home first. I only have to make it a few more miles, but there's no way I can command the steering wheel if I cannot get my tremors under control.

Stupid Fintan, making me so stressed I can't calm my own body down.

When I come to a stop light, I flex my fingers and shake them out. Poor Rome is worried. He tells me he needs me to stay on the phone with him until I get home.

When a fist bangs on my window, I scream. Then I growl in frustration when Rome demands to know what scared me. "It's just Declan. Hold on." I roll down my window, scowling at my brother, who is standing at my car door in the rain at the empty intersection. "You scared the crap out of me. What's wrong?"

"Let's park your car at the store up there, and I'll drive you the rest of the way."

"No, Declan. I'm fine."

"Tell me that all you want, but I could feel your tremors starting when I was holding your hand back at Dad's house. Do you have your medicine?"

I cringe that my brother feels the need to check on my meds, as if I am still a child. "It's at home." The rain drips into my car and dots my skin. I can see the droplets on my arm, but I'm starting to lose feeling in my extremities.

I hate it when this happens.

If I'd been taking my pills regularly, the descent

wouldn't be this fast, or it wouldn't happen at all. I curse myself for deciding this was the week to try weaning myself off my medication.

Declan doesn't lose his jaunty personality just because he is scared and being rained on. "If I was Fintan, I'd get all sarcastic and say, 'Well, that's a good place for it.' But I'm not a jerk, so I'll just suggest again that we pull over so I can drive you the rest of the way."

I shake my head, unwilling to bend. It's a matter of wills—me against Fintan, and now me against my body. "It's just a few more miles. I'll pull over if it gets bad."

Declan's eyes fall to my arms, which are visibly quaking. "No, you wont." He doesn't point out with words that it's already on its way to bad. "Best hurry up, if it's this intense already. I'm right behind you."

I swallow hard, clinging to the truth in his words. "Love you, Declan."

"Love you, Coco-bean."

I roll up my window, my hand slipping on the button twice before I am able to shut out the rain.

Rome's voice is low and deadly. "What medicine? Coletta, what is Declan talking about? What tremors?"

I chew on my lower lip, holding back the stream of cussing I am ready to unleash on the world for being this cruel. "That's family stuff you don't need to worry about."

And just like that, I have demoted Rome from boyfriend to acquaintance. No way would I tolerate not knowing something important about his health, yet I am expecting him to turn a blind eye to my situation because... because...

...because I don't want my condition to be true.

...because I don't want Rome to look at me like I am anything less than amazing and capable.

...because this is hard and embarrassing, and I don't want him to see my problems that might never go away.

I don't want him to see me incapacitated.

I don't want him to know there were whole years where I couldn't walk without assistance.

Sweat beads on the nape of my neck. What if this never goes away? What if I can't wean myself off my medication? What if the best I can do comes with limitations?

Rome doesn't yell, but there is a deadly quality to his voice that makes me flinch. "Do you think I am playing around? I'm not in this so I can make out with you and leave you to deal with the hard stuff on your own. I want to be completely in your life, not on the periphery, only looking at the pleasant parts."

I don't know how to respond, so for a span of time, I don't. I expect Rome to fill in the silence, but he waits me out until I finally crack. "It's nothing. They're psychogenetic tremors. It's nothing we need to talk about. It's all PTSD crap that I dealt with years ago. Every now and then I have flareups, like when Fintan gets on his high horse and tries to bully me into hiding again. I'm really, really fine, and I really, really don't want to talk about it."

Again, silence fills the car, but this time, Rome is the one who finally speaks. "What helps you when this happens? What's the medicine?"

I hate that we are talking about this. My jaw firms as I tell him the name of my pills.

"We're not going to our spot tomorrow. We'll do it another day."

I grit my teeth when my hands slip on the steering wheel. "No! See, this is why I don't need you to know. I can handle myself. I don't need to cancel my plans. I'll be fine in a minute."

"How?"

"Sheer force of will!" I shout, more at my muscles than at him.

Rome doesn't comment on my asinine reply. Instead, he keeps his voice calm. "I'm making you upset. How about I tell you about my day. Would that be a good distraction?"

"Yes. Yes, please. Let's talk about anything but this."

"I learned again that Nico is a terrible shot. He was aiming at a target and hit the one next to it."

I let out a humorless laugh. "Might want to take him shooting at the range more often for practice."

"Maybe. He's distracted lately. We got into it this morning." Rome fills the rest of my drive home with the back and forth between Nico and himself, which is the typical brother stuff. Even when you add in guns and high vampiric stakes, it's still familial bickering at its finest. I miss being witness to the Valentino dysfunctionality. Makes my family seem almost normal.

"Tell me you're home," Rome says when his story ends.

"Pulling onto my street now, as a matter of fact. See? I told you; I'm fine. Nothing I can't handle, and nothing you need to worry about. I'm going to hang up now, okay? Declan's going to do a walk through my house before he leaves. I'm pretty sure he won't enjoy the sultry sound of your voice as much as I do."

"Fair enough. Colette?"

"Yes?"

"I wish you would have told me about this."

I chew on my lower lip, concentrating hard to keep my grip on the steering wheel. "I know. I'm sorry, I…"

"You don't need to apologize. We're still new to each other. We'll get there. But if you're wondering if I want to know this stuff, I do. The big things and the little ones."

I speak to him through gritted teeth when it becomes clear to me that my fingers are completely useless. "I'll try to remember that."

"I'm on my way to you."

My intake of breath is loud, but the scandal rings through my car even louder. "That is the worst idea in the world. You are not crossing territory lines. You'll put yourself in danger if anyone in the East End spots your very recognizable car."

"I'm on my way. I was already in Midtown, so I'm halfway there. I'll borrow a car from one of my people, so I won't be spotted."

"This is taking things too far, Rome!" The more worked up I get, the harder it is to control my hands. I'm squeezing the steering wheel so tight, I am afraid I might bend the thing. But I know if I let go, I won't be able to get a good grip again.

My forearms are trembling, the muscles jumping so much, I accidentally veer to the wrong side of the road. A sharp scream belts out through my gritted teeth as I right the car, narrowly avoiding oncoming traffic.

"What happened? Colette, pull over! I'll come and get you."

"No! I can do this by myself. I didn't hit anything. Declan's behind me. It's fine. I'm normal."

I repeat the mantra to myself over and over.

I'm normal.

I don't have PTSD.

I don't have random attacks where my tremors are so bad, I cannot control my own body.

I don't have a brain injury.

I'm normal.

"Pull over!" The command in his voice is hard to ignore, but I am my father's daughter to a fault, so I push out his advice and keep on my unsteady course until I pull into my driveway with a gust of relief.

"I'm home. I did it. Goodnight, Rome." I end the call when he is mid-cussing because, at the end of the day, no matter how much we care about each other, Rome will never see my home. He will never know this side of me because I keep it buried in the East End, where vampires are not allowed to traverse.

I never want him to see me like this. I want him to know that I am strong and willful, beautiful and capable.

I don't want him to see me unable to walk in a straight line.

I paw at my door, unable to grip the handle to let myself out of my own vehicle. Panic strangles me around the throat because I know it's only going to get worse from here.

No. This is part of me that Rome will never see.

17

TWO PILLS, TOO LATE
COLETTE

*D*eclan takes his time roaming through my house, even going so far as checking under my bed for monsters, like he did when I was little. "I am not leaving until you take your pill," he warns, pulling my bottle of pills from my medicine cabinet and plopping the container atop my living room coffee table. "You know it's too late for your daily medicine to do its thing. You have to take the tranquilizer."

My home is beautiful. Everything was selected with the utmost purpose and care. The coffee table is sage colored with a glass top. The soft green matches the gold accents of the hearth and the glowing lights I installed behind my mounted television. Everything is sage and cream in my living room, with sporadic touches of lavender and gold throughout. It's perfect.

But the bright orange bottle of tranquilizers on the

table in the center of the living room sticks out as something that truly does not belong in my home.

Declan crosses his arms over his chest. "Now, Coco. You're in bad shape. This isn't the time for your denial."

"I d-d-don't want to t-t-take the tranquilizer." I know I sound petulant, but I don't care. "I d-d-don't like the way it makes me f-f-feel. I c-c-can't even get up the stairs once it kicks in."

"You should have thought of that before you skipped your meds today. Don't think I can't tell when you do that, because I can. Did you run out?"

"No. I was trying to t-t-take them less often."

Declan's cadence turns slow and deep with menace. "How less often?"

I wish I could feel my fingers. "Twice a week."

Declan swears, starting and stopping several lectures as he splutters his dismay. "We're not getting into how dangerous that is, Coco."

"Good. Because it's my b-b-body."

"Your brain needs that medicine! If you go downhill, it affects me. Don't you get that? Without you, all I have is the sheriff and stupid Fintan! If you don't care about yourself enough to take your pills, then care about me! I can't handle this family without you."

I examine my brother and see his palpable pain. It's not just because he is worried about me; there is something deeper there that haunts him.

Before I can say anything, he holds up his hands, taking a steadying breath. "Whatever. You're not doing that again, correct? You see that your meds are necessary, right?"

It's an effort, but I manage a mortified, "Yeah, okay."

"Good. Now you're taking two pills—your daily med and your tranquilizer. You have your day off tomorrow, so you don't have to worry about doing stuff. Take them now, Coco. I'm serious. Don't make me get all authoritative on you. You know I hate having to sound like Fintan or the sheriff. It increases the chance of me getting a bald spot to match Dad's."

I snigger, but the pain of my muscles jumping for this long cuts short any chance at levity.

I hate this.

"I'll help you up the stairs," Declan offers. "I know you're worried about that."

Flashes of my nurse having to help me bathe, having to walk me from the bedroom to the dining room, having to help me on the toilet all flood my mind.

Instinctively, I recoil from Declan's offer.

He's a good person, a good brother, but I am a stubborn woman and a prideful sister. "No. I would s-s-sooner die. I can do it m-m-myself."

We both know I can't, but Declan is polite enough not to call me on it. "Okay. You can sleep down here, I guess.

But I am not leaving until you take both pills. You know this won't go away on its own."

"Maybe it w-will," I argue, my voice quavering that much more.

He hands me my daily pill that won't do me much good now. I'm too far gone for it to do more than steady me after I wake from the tranquilizer.

Still, I toss it back. "See? I'm b-b-better already."

Crap. When I can't keep my voice steady, that's a checkpoint I don't like to cross.

Declan makes a show of sitting on my cream leather couch, spreading out his arms to make himself comfortable. "Don't think I can't hear you stuttering. You know you need the tranquilizer. You will kick yourself into a full-blown seizure, and I'm not having that."

I give him a nice shot of my middle finger, but the effect is compromised, because my hand is shaking too badly to look truly menacing. At least I remembered to kick my heels off at the door. Sometimes I forget, and I end up falling when my legs go numb.

How I wish this wasn't something I've grown used to.

"Fine!" I don't like that I am raising my voice at Declan, but that's the volume that cracks out of me when I am this embarrassed. I don't want to be a woman who doesn't have full control over her body. That's just about the worst thing that can happen to a girl.

On top of that, it's all I can do to block out the reason I

am this way. I can already smell the phantom stink of cement stinging my nose. I can hear the footsteps coming toward me with grim purpose.

My arms start to itch, but when I try to scratch them, I only end up hitting myself because my fingers are pretty much useless as far as dexterity goes.

Declan unscrews the lid and stands, taking out a single pill that I hate with every fiber of my being. I don't want this help, this admission that I cannot handle things on my own.

But I know Declan won't let up. In the back of my mind, the warning is coming that soon I won't be able to breathe properly.

I really don't like going through that.

Then the seizure that can be catastrophic might peek its head around the corner. The last time I had one of those, I lost speech for three weeks.

I can't go back to that. I won't. I have too much to say now—too much to accomplish.

I reach for the pill with utter defeat in my soul, but I only end up knocking it to the floor. "Oh! I didn't mean to d-d-do that."

"I know. It's okay, Coco." Declan doesn't take offense. He gets down on his knees and fishes the pill out from under the couch.

My legs are unsteady now. The tremors are moving

faster than I anticipated. When they hit my legs, I have to lie down, or I'll fall.

I guess I'm not getting off the couch tonight.

"D-Declan," I whimper, sounding just as pathetic as I feel.

"I'm right here. There it is. Jeez, that little sucker rolled far."

Declan is on his knees still when a voice that shoots hope and simultaneous dread through my body calls from the side entrance. "Coletta? Tré-sur, I'm here."

A sob cracks out of me because it's too late. It's too late for the tranquilizer to do what it's supposed to without a few sizeable hiccups.

It's too late for me to shield Declan from knowing that I have been sneaking around with Rome.

It's too late for me to explain things to Declan. He draws the gun from his belt and stands. My amiable best friend is gone, and in his place stands a defender of Kennedy territory.

TOO LATE

COLETTE

*M*y voice is choppy and not as commanding as I need it to be when Rome breaks into my house at exactly the wrong moment. "No! No, D-Declan!"

Declan has his gun aimed at Rome, who has picked his way through the lock on the side of my house. "Don't move, Rome!" Declan is glaring with his upper lip curled, which isn't a look I like to see on my brother. "What are you doing here, man? You're way off your territory, coming to Colette's house like this."

Though Rome has carried a gun on him since he was a young teenager, he doesn't reach for it. His hands raise in surrender, which I know is a difficult position for him to take. He is dressed in his normal black slacks and white dress shirt with the cuffs rolled, but there is a long red stain along the length of his right arm.

Is he hurt?

"I came here because Colette isn't feeling well. I'm guessing we're here for the same reason."

"I'm here to protect her. I cannot imagine why *you're* here." Declan doesn't lower his gun.

So much for the friendship that was rebuilding between them.

With every second that passes, my anxiety ramps up higher. My tremors are impossible to hide. I want to run away from both of the men I adore. I want to run away from myself and this problem that flares up at the most inopportune times. My legs are unstable and barely useable to keep me upright, but I struggle to stand all the same.

I can't feel my legs.

No matter. I just won't walk.

"Declan, put the gun d-d-d..." I cannot finish my sentence. Tears smart my eyes with a mix of humiliation and fear.

Rome keeps his distance with his hands raised. When his eyes meet mine, sheer agony screams out from them. "I'm here because I love your sister. Keep me at gunpoint all you like, but if Colette is in trouble, I'm not going to leave her wellbeing to chance."

Declan pales, shock overcoming him. He shakes his head as if that will rid him of Rome's declaration.

Of course the moment Rome tells me he loves me is

when he is held at gunpoint. And of course it's way too soon for either of us to be feeling this.

That doesn't make it any less true, though. I feel it, too, this connection that's unshakable no matter how horrible an idea it may be.

Declan doesn't lower his weapon. "Back up, Valentino. Don't stop talking until you start making sense."

Rome swallows hard, not looking at Declan as he speaks. He meets my eyes with unmitigated devotion. "Your sister and I have been seeing each other in secret for a few months. We didn't plan it, but we can't stop it, either." Then to me, he says, "You sounded scared, like you were hurt. What happened, tré-sur?"

I cannot bring myself to tell him all that is wrong with me. This is supposed to be the new love phase, where everything is happy and fun and flirty. I don't want him to see me like this.

I don't want to *be* like this.

"You're hurt," I say instead, switching the subject from me to him. I try to motion to the blood on his shirt, but my hand is quaking too badly to be useful.

Rome's chin moves from left to right. "Barely a scratch." His brows push together, taking in my trembling with rapt fascination. "Why are you shaking?"

Declan finally lowers his gun but doesn't holster the thing. "Is this true, Colette?"

My brother rarely calls me by my full name.

I try to nod, but my body is quaking so badly, I'm not sure my response is noticeable. It's discomfort on top of humiliation.

I didn't want my brother to find out like this.

I didn't want him to find out at all.

"What's happening to her?" Rome asks Declan, surpassing my input because it must be obvious that I cannot communicate clearly anymore.

Declan finally holsters his weapon, thank goodness.

I am so relieved that my boyfriend might not get shot before my very eyes that elation spreads through my body. I step forward to embrace Rome as a sob of need bursts out of me.

My legs want to move toward him, but they don't remember how. My knee gives up the fight of holding me upright, and my whole body crashes to the floor.

Everything hurts on a new level now. My chin slams on the floor and my wrist smacks the coffee table on my way down.

Still, the quaking won't relent.

Declan swears as he rushes to my side, lifting my upper half in his arms. It's harder than it would be if my limbs would just cooperate, but I am spasming with no semblance of control.

Declan is no stranger to my condition. He plops his butt on my cream carpet, pulling me onto his lap. "Get the bottle on the table there. She needs her pills."

I want to tell them both to get out of here, to leave me alone so no one has to see me like this. I am humiliated and completely devoid of control or grace. But when I try to open my mouth to say exactly that, I realize my jaw isn't functioning as it should.

A frustrated scream belts out of me.

"Open up, Coco," Declan pleads, but we both know I have lost control of my body. Even if I wanted to comply, I couldn't. "You shouldn't be here!" my brother roars at Rome, who kneels on my other side, bottle in hand.

"How many?" Rome asks, ignoring any notes of hostility.

"One, but *I* have to give it to her. You don't know how to do it."

Rome doesn't argue. When my eyes roll back in my head, perhaps he senses that no matter what traditional help he might want to offer, this has surpassed the normal level of a layman's medical know-how.

I hate this part. Why didn't I take my pill today? Darn my stupid pride.

Declan pins my arms down with his forearm and then reaches around me to pinch my cheeks so my mouth opens. Tears smart my eyes because this isn't the first time my brother has had to do this for me.

My doctor warned me this would happen. He told me that he didn't recommend me going back home, especially since it would be my first time living alone.

I am twenty-five years old. I should be able to live on my own.

But the stupid yet solid logic of me being in danger of relapsing if my tremors take over and turn to seizures is not something I can always shrug off.

On Declan's instruction, Rome pries open my jaw and slips a pill between my teeth. Declan knows I am past the point of being able to control my throat, so he goes for the old tried and true.

My panic hits a new level when his hand covers my mouth. He tells Rome to pinch my nose.

It feels like I am drowning, fighting for breath while my airways are shut off.

Rome is shouting in fright while Declan shouts back. The both of them panic until my swallow reflex finally kicks in, and the pill slides down my throat.

It's not instantaneous, but no more than a minute goes by before the tension in my limbs begins to release.

What started out as a hold mutates quickly into a hug. My brother rocks me in his arms as my limbs go slack and my head drops into the crook of his arm.

"Easy, Coco-bean. Everything is okay." Declan's short, light brown waves fall forward, his eyes glistening with worry. "See? We just have to work on our timing. We waited too long."

It's a good brother, the one who doesn't call you out on your ruined pride.

Though the very real dread that Rome is seeing me like this is not gone from my mind, as the medicine travels through me, I find there is precious little that bothers me at all anymore.

I can see Rome's terror, but it doesn't register more than a blip as my lashes flutter and then begin to close. He calls my name over and over, but all I can think is that he's here. Everything will somehow be okay because Rome is with me.

I tell myself all sorts of lies seconds before I pass out.

19

BROTHER AND BOYFRIEND
ROME

I am in desperate need of sleep and a shower, but I know neither of those things will find me tonight. If Declan thinks he can send me home, I have clearly underplayed how much I love his sister.

I hate that I said it at gunpoint.

Part of me hates that I said it at all, but that doesn't make it any less true.

I motion between Declan and myself. "Look, you and I can fight about this all you want. The bottom line is that this is Colette's home. Only she can order me out of it."

Declan exhales with such drama that he spits a little on the coffee table. "Do you hear yourself? All I have to do is call my father, and you're behind bars. You do realize you're a vampire, right? This is the East End. You're not allowed to cross territory lines."

My upper lip curls. "Do *you* hear *yourself*? How

outdated is that law? If there is peace in the city, as everyone claims, then it shouldn't be a problem if I drive to my girlfriend's house."

Declan speaks through gritted teeth. "I swear, I am this close to losing it. Don't push me. My sister is not your girlfriend."

"She absolutely is. Why else would I be here?"

Declan doesn't bother keeping his voice low as he paces between the coffee table and the television; it's clear Coletta is out cold. "I have no idea, okay? You're not her boyfriend because I'm her *best* friend. I would have known about you."

I chuckle, though there is no joy in the sound. "And how would you have reacted? Yelling and putting her on a short leash? Holding me at gunpoint? Think again if she really would have told you something like the two of us getting together."

I can tell my logic has hit a nerve. Declan's shoulders deflate, though it is clear he still hates me. "Why didn't she tell me? How did this even happen?"

It's not asked with the intrigue of a best friend wanting all the details; Declan uses the grave tone of one addressing a natural disaster when discussing the two of us pairing up.

I motion to Coletta's form. I don't like the sight of her laid out on the couch, lifeless with her lips parted. She's a beauty, but without that fire that forces her to argue the world's finer points, her loveliness isn't the same. "If you're going to call the sheriff, go ahead. I'm not here to do anything other than help Colette. She didn't sound like herself on the phone, so I dropped everything, traded my car with a friend's and came straight here. Any law that keeps me from being good to my girlfriend isn't one I'm going to lose sleep over."

I need to sit down. I am exhausted, and I can tell this is going to be a long night.

I'm not trying to start a whole new fight by picking up Colette's upper half and sliding my body onto the couch, but I know any move I make is a risk. I straighten my spine and rest her head across my lap.

Tensions are high. I am not worried about besting Declan in a fight. That is, if I was willing to fight him. I know that if Declan throws a punch, I won't be retaliating. My little cannoli would be horrified to see us come to blows.

"Dangerous ground," Declan warns me, but he doesn't intervene other than that.

I move slowly, my fingers pulling through Coletta's long, dark waves. "Her forehead is warm. Does she have an ice pack in the fridge?"

"She does, but I'm not leaving you alone with her, not even for a second."

"What danger do you imagine I am to her? She's far more a danger to me."

Declan's words come out slowly. "Then why are you here? I cannot wrap my mind around you sitting in my sister's house."

I don't like jostling Coletta again, but her forehead is too warm for my liking. "I'll get the ice pack, then." I'm careful with her, cradling her head gently until it's laid back on the couch.

I am a stranger in her home.

I don't have a favorite cup here.

I don't know where she keeps the vacuum.

I don't even know at what temperature she keeps her thermostat.

I don't like the way that feels.

Everything is new to me: the bright color scheme in the hallway with a portrait of her family back when she was younger, hanging beside a sole portrait of her mother, back when the woman was still alive. I haven't seen a picture of Mama Kennedy in ages, but looking at her now, I see traces of her daughter in her fiery eyes and wavy chocolate hair that does what it feels like.

Colette's kitchen is in order, but for the dishes that still need to be done and the dough that's rising on the counter.

She was going to bake bread. Of course she was. My girl likes doing things herself, rather than rely on the easy way of living one's life.

Her kitchen has subdued green accents against white

appliances. Everything is clean and put together, but I can tell it's not lived in all that often.

She works long hours, just like me.

I have to dig around for her ice pack in the freezer.

My spine straightens when my hand lands on a dagger wrapped in a cloth.

What the...

She's afraid. She's got a dagger in her freezer, which is a strange place to hide such a thing. It tells me she must have other weapons hidden around the house.

Part of me is grateful she knows how to protect herself.

The other part of me knows I am not going anywhere if she is this worried.

20

WOUNDS AND WOUNDED PRIDE
ROME

When I make my way back to the living room with an ice pack in my hand, Declan eyes me with less hostility and a clear increase in curiosity. "I don't know what to make of this," he admits.

"That's okay. I didn't either, at first. Now I'm in too deep to care. Your sister sneezes twice, and I'm near ready to have a heart attack."

"You crossed into our territory for her. This is serious, Valentino."

It doesn't bother me that he addresses me by my last name, but it's a clear gauntlet thrown that we are not friends in this situation.

I expected as much.

I am careful with Colette as I lift her upper half once more and slide onto the couch so I can rest her head on my lap. The cold pack lays across her forehead.

The sight of it tugs at my heart. I don't like seeing her less than fierce. She would be upset if I saw her like this.

I know this because she's a lot like me.

I keep my eyes on her face while I speak. "I'm well past serious. But I didn't know about this. What happened to her? Is it seizures?"

Declan folds his arms across his chest, standing on the other side of the coffee table from us. "It turns into seizures if she doesn't take her pills regularly, which she didn't do this week. Normally her daily meds keep her condition under control. When things get real bad, like tonight, I have to give her a tranquilizer. She doesn't like the tranquilizer because it does this to her. Takes her body down to zero so it doesn't overload. She's going to be pretty much useless for at least twelve hours now. Sometimes longer."

"I need the name of it, Declan. The actual diagnosis." I'm going to be conducting quite the internet search when I get home.

The pause before Declan answers is so long, I worry I will have to beat the information out of him, which I know I cannot do.

"It's a combination of things." Declan runs his hand through his wavy hair. I can tell he's nervous at ratting out his sister to me. "It's a little of her genetics. You know my mother died at age thirty, and she was on her way out that whole last year of her life. Her muscles began to atrophy, which is eventually what will happen to Colette." He swallows hard. I can see it is an effort to speak clinically about the horrors his sister will have to endure. "But she has medicine our mother did not, so our hope is that she will live longer with fewer limitations. Her genetics aren't the main factor here."

I motion to Colette's form. "You call this not a main factor? She is completely incapacitated!"

Declan keeps his cadence calm. "What you're seeing tonight is a combination of things. Yes, her genetics, but this is largely PTSD from all the times she was abducted, coupled with the side effects of her brain injury. Mostly the brain injury. But one feeds the other."

A stream of cussing floods my mind and accidentally spills out of my mouth. "Her *what*?" I finally manage. My entire world slows until those two words are my only focus.

My girlfriend's condition is far worse than I could have imagined.

"That's not possible," I argue. "Orlando saved her from that basement the last time she was abducted. He saved her. She doesn't have a brain injury."

"Yes, Orlando saved her life, but a lot of damage was already done. She won't tell me what they did to her, but it was bad. Bad enough that she was in a wheelchair for a while."

My mouth falls open at the image I cannot force to make sense. "How did I not know any of this?"

Declan runs his hand over his face. "None of us knows the extent of any of it. As soon as it was safe for her to fly, our father put her on a plane and flew her to Lonmure, where she was kept inside with a nurse to take care of her. All doctors and nurses and OTs and PTs came to her house to help her get back on her feet. She disappeared from the news for several years. Eventually finished high school from her house."

I am at a loss, usure how my world cracked open so horribly without warning. "I didn't know any of this."

I can tell Declan doesn't want to be talking about Colette's condition, and not just because it's me on the listening end.

He keeps his gaze from me as he speaks. "That last time she was taken—the time Orlando rescued her—she tried to escape one too many times, I guess. They beat her over the head until she passed out. Orlando found her and got her out, but after that, she wasn't the same. The rehab took years, and even now, there are parts of her that will never be back how they were." He motions to her hands. "Whenever she doesn't take her meds regularly, she gets the shakes. Add panic to that, add nerves to that, and it goes south real quick. Sometimes it's so bad that her throat closes up and she can't breathe."

Another flood of cussing fills my brain. "How is this the first time I'm hearing about it?"

Declan scoffs in my direction. "How is this the first time *I'm* hearing about *you*?"

Fair point.

"Then why is she putting herself through the stress of opening a business in Midtown? That seems against doctor's orders, if you ask me."

"No kidding. Try telling her to back down from anything; I dare you. She's not supposed to do high stress activities. She's not supposed to live alone. And I highly doubt she should be the one holding scissors to someone's head in the event she gets the shakes at work. But it's like the second the doctor told her how limited her mobility would be, her fighting nature went into overdrive."

I give a joyless, one-noted laugh. "That sounds about right."

Because it's exactly how I would react to being given limitations. My little cannoli and I are the same.

Declan keeps his eyes on the coffee table. "So she can walk up the stairs now. In heels, no less. She learned to feed herself again. Learned how to live without assistance. Got her driver's license back. She purposefully chose a job where you need steady hands." He snorts. "I don't even know if she likes doing hair, or if she chose it to prove her doctors wrong."

I cannot picture any of this. She is only twenty-five.

I run my hand over my face, incorporating the new information into the beginnings of a plan. Before I can truly work things through, I'm thinking aloud. "Then she'll move in with me." I shake my head as new logic sprouts up. "No. Nico would be a problem. I'll move in here, then."

Declan's mouth drops open as if I've said something crazy. "How long have you even been dating?"

I shrug. "A few months. I'm pretty sure I would've made the same decision a week in, though." When Declan still regards me with that dopey expression, I smooth Coletta's hair back. "Who did it? Who hurt her? When Orlando and I got through the mess of revolutionaries, she was alone in the basement there. Did we kill them all?"

Declan leans down and situates himself on the floor because Colette and I are taking up the entire length of the couch. He picks at his nails while he talks to me. "We don't know. The sheriff thinks a few split before we got there, and she can't remember their faces. Her shrink says it's repressed memory syndrome or something."

"Human or vampire?"

"What do you think?"

Declan won't say it aloud, but I know it was their side who did this. It always is. In all the times she's been snatched at, it's never been from my side. Vampires tend to give her a wide berth, steering clear so she doesn't accidentally bleed on us.

"Tell me the extent of the damage. If there's more, I want to know it." Though truly, I'm not sure I will ever be ready to hear it. She is important to me, more than a human should be, even entwined as our families have always been.

And she didn't tell me about this. She didn't tell me a thing.

Declan rubs the nape of his neck. "I probably shouldn't. She'll be mad I snitched."

The corner of my mouth lifts because it's a true sign of Declan being willing to work with me on this, instead of against. "I can't help her if I don't have the information."

Declan's chin lowers in defeat. "Whoever it was that beat her around the head did a good job of disappearing, I'll tell you that. If I could have found them, I already would have. That was Dad's last straw. As soon as she was vaguely coherent, he sent her overseas to get her out of Mayfield. I'm not sure she's forgiven him for that. He set her up with a nurse who lived with her and made sure she was seeing the doctor regularly." Declan motions around the immaculately clean house. "This is the first time she's been allowed to live on her own. She's gone a whole year without an episode. We were hoping the bulk of it was behind her, but even so, we told her not to come back here. Stress triggers a lot of what the medication tries to fend off."

"Which is?"

"It's a traumatic brain injury, Valentino. It affected just about everything she did in the beginning. She's come a long way. It's almost a non-issue if she takes her medication every day. But she just told me that she skipped a few days to wean herself off it. Poor decision on her part, plus the whole thing worsens when she gets overloaded. Why do you think we've been harping on her not to open her shop in Midtown? We know just as well as she does that it's going to trigger some major overload."

I fight the urge to gather Coletta's limp form up in my arms and run her clear out of the city. "What was the trigger tonight?"

Was it me? Is dating me one too many things?

And if it is, could I summon up enough unselfishness in me to bow out?

I don't want to look that problem in the eye if I don't have to, so I hold my breath while Declan decides how he wants to word his reply.

"Fintan found a note on the front door of the salon. It's the revolution, threatening to abduct her again." Declan's head hangs as he curls his knees up, wrappings his arms around his shins. He looks younger like that. I can picture him trying to tag along with Fintan and me on our less than savory missions. More often than not, Declan was shunted to watch Colette and Nico. No doubt that's how the two of them became so close.

I fish for my phone, careful not to jostle the angel on my lap too much. I pull up the picture I snapped of the letter I found taped to the salon's front door a couple months ago and display it to Declan. "Something like this?"

Declan's mouth pops open. His eyebrows push together as the same dread that's creeping in my veins races through his. "When did that happen?"

"It didn't, as far as your sister knows. I saw it the first time I went to visit her to congratulate her on her new business, but I took it with me, so she never saw it. I figured she didn't need that kind of stress opening week."

"You figured right. Any idea who put it there?"

"Not yet. I was going to wait until she trusted me a little more before I asked her if I could put surveillance cameras outside her building. I'm new at relationships, but I'm guessing that's not something she'll agree to before she's told me she loves me without taking it back in the next breath."

Declan snorts at the two of us. "She loves you."

Even though it's not coming from her, I can't help the swell of happiness that hits my chest.

"She hid you from me." Declan taps the side of his fist to his chest. "My sister only does stuff like that when it's too close to the vest to share. She tells me about the stupid dates all the time. But the salon? She didn't tell me until she'd already signed the lease. She hides the things that make her vulnerable." He motions to his sister. "Kinda like how she hid her condition from you."

"Vulnerability isn't the same thing as love," I argue, though I'm not sure why I don't just take the win and run.

Declan stares at his knees, looking like he's got a million things on his mind. "To us it is."

I let his wisdom settle in my mind while my fingers comb through Colette's hair. I want to throw a parade because the only woman who has been able to hold my attention for more than a single date might actually love me in return without taking it back in a fit of panic.

I keep my backside parked where it is, knowing we will need to take everything slower than either of us would like.

My fingers bunch in her hair. "How do I take care of her?"

"First off, never phrase it like that. She'll straight up kick you out if you imply she needs to be taken care of."

I chuckle silently. "Understood."

Declan takes his time running me through how to administer the tranquilizer, which is for emergencies only. I fight back my horror as he explains all the different levels of disrepair I might find her in, and what to do in each scenario. With every explanation, I can feel her pride withering, even though she is unconscious and unaware we are talking about her. Still, I know her pride like I know my own.

When Declan finishes filling me in, the silence that settles between us isn't as uncomfortable as I assumed it would be. He and I were never really close, but we played baseball in the backyard together, spent summers at the lake, and enjoyed all the other perks of having parents who used to be best friends before greed and life got the better of them.

"Dad isn't going to like this," Declan whispers. It's as if he is afraid that no matter where he is in the world, his father can hear him.

I had the same caution regarding my own father, back when he was alive.

I use my free hand to text Orlando and tell him to procure a bottle of Colette's medicine for me to keep at my place in case she ever runs out.

"I'm not worried about the sheriff," I say to Declan. "I'm worried about you." I don't realize how true those words are until they pop out without me checking them first. I settle into the couch, leaning my head back as I comb my hand over Colette's hair. I can't stop petting her. "Colette loves you. If you hate me, it'll be hard on her. So tell me now how to make this work, and I'll do it."

Declan sighs, shaking his head. He stares at us as if trying to force the odd visual in front of him to make sense. "Don't tell the sheriff, for starters. If you value the treaty at all, dating his daughter isn't the way to show it."

"I think we should come clean, but it's Colette's family, so it's her call. She seems to be on the same wavelength as you."

"Good. At least she hasn't lost her mind entirely." Declan casts me a disparaging look, and I can't say I blame him. I shouldn't have left the raid just because Colette sounded off.

I should tend to my arm, which stings from the flesh wound I sustained in the fight.

I should leave the East End.

There are a lot of things I *should* do, but none of them matter anymore. I want to be here when she wakes. I have to make sure she's alright, even if it means leaving the life I thought was important behind.

21

FATHER KNOWS BEST
ROME

When Coletta's phone rings, I lean over to silence it, so as not to wake her. Her father's name on the screen is logged in as The Sheriff.

I don't understand their relationship. They don't fight, not that I can tell, at least. But the formalities and verbal distance are odd to parse through.

"Your dad is calling Colette," I tell Declan, who roused at the sound.

"Huh? What time is it?"

"Declan, go sleep in Colette's bed. Sleeping on the floor can't be comfortable."

Declan sits up, rubbing his eyes. He made himself a spot with a blanket and a throw pillow partway through the night on the living room floor. It's barely eight in the morning. Light is streaming through the gaps in the curtains.

Declan stretches his arms over his head. "I'm not sleeping in her room. I'm not leaving the two of you alone."

I get it, but I don't like the implications that I can't be trusted to look after the woman I adore.

Declan's phone rings. "Hey, Dad."

I still so I can hear both ends of the conversation as best as I am able. The room is quiet, so I can make out enough of the sheriff's voice, which has never learned to whisper.

"Have you heard from Coco? She's supposed to be here."

"Be where?"

"At City Hall. We have an interview with the press scheduled for eight o'clock so I can get it done with before we all go to work. There are about fifteen reporters here, ready to aim their questions at the mayor and the two of us, but she's not here."

Declan grimaces as he glances at his sister's supine form. Last night he said that the tranquilizer knocks her out for a solid twelve hours, and we're not nearly to the end of that.

Sure enough, even the talking right in front of her doesn't disturb her slumber.

She looks like an angel, her brunette hair fanned out over the throw pillow on my lap. After Declan nodded off last night, I contented myself running my fingers through her waves, loving the vanilla scent that unleashed itself into the air just to taunt me with its allure.

Her lips are slightly parted—plump and perfect as they always are. She is a fairytale come to life, and I get to watch over her while she rests.

Declan pinches the bridge of his nose. "I'm sorry. Yeah, she isn't feeling herself. I think all the work at the park caught up with her. Then the note Fintan's friend found taped to the salon's door sent her over the edge. She had a flareup last night, so I had to give her a pill."

The sheriff's questions come out in a stream of worry. "What do you mean? Is she at the hospital? Do we need to call her doctor?"

"We?" Declan snorts. "Come on, Dad. You know I'm the only one who checks on her status. I'll call the doctor once she's awake. I don't do things like that behind her back."

"You should call the doctor now. If I did it, I wouldn't understand half the stuff he says. You speak that language because you're a medic."

Declan is just tired enough to correct his father. "No, I understand her doctor because I've been in this from day one, checking on her and getting reports on the regular."

I can tell this truth makes the sheriff uncomfortable. "Yeah, yeah. Fine. Let me know what the doctor says."

"Will do. I don't know what to tell you about the press conference. She's out cold. She can't come in."

The sheriff sighs. He sounds so old when he does that.

"It is what it is. Mayor Stapleton is going to take all the credit for her ideas, her plan, her rallying everyone to make this happen. The parks are finished. She deserves the photo op."

Declan chuckles. "You know she prefers it that way. She only demanded the spotlight to make the mayor sweat and push him into action."

"I know. But just once, I want to see that bastard squirm."

Declan's pleasant demeanor comes naturally. "I'll put that on your Christmas list."

"Tell Coco not to worry about the press conference. I'll handle the media."

"I'll consider it off her plate."

When Declan ends the call, he treats me to a sidelong glance. "I could have taken that call in the other room, you know."

"But you chose to answer it in front of me, where I could hear everything. Either you trust me, or you want me to know your sister better—the parts of her she hides."

"A little of both, I suppose. Though, I'm not sure trust is the right word. I want you to be good for her." He runs his fingers through his light brown hair, making it even more disheveled. "Really, I want to know nothing about the two of you. But I know my sister. She did this for you. This whole fixing up the parks agenda was because she cares about you. So you should see what goes on behind the scenes when she sticks her neck out for you."

I smash my lips shut. That is exactly the reason she kicked the revamp of the parks into high gear. I was whining to her about a problem that I couldn't fix, so she up and solved it for me in the best way possible. She made sure other people stepped in and did what they knew they should have been doing all along. Coletta inspired them to action because she cares about me.

Declan's jaw ticks with frustration. "She doesn't do things halfway. What you're playing at isn't a little fling. It's a big deal when she jumps all in. Taking a risk like this? Being with you? She's all in. There's no way she's going to hold herself back now."

"Why are you telling me this?"

Declan turns his head toward me. "Because you should walk away. If you actually care about her, you should end things." He motions to her form. "This secret isn't something she can sustain. It's going to come out and she's going to take the hit for it. She always does. People watch her like a hawk, wanting to know what the Last Deadblood is up to. What sort of toothpaste does she use? What shoes is she wearing today? There was a full spread done on the blind date Fintan set her up with last month, and the date barely lasted an hour."

"I know all of that. We're keeping things secret."

Declan scoffs at my naïveté. "Please tell me you are not

this stupid. A vampire lurking in the East End is not the way to keep anything secret. This is going to come out. Stuff like this always does."

I hold her closer, lifting her torso in my arms as if Declan means to snatch her away from me. "If I could walk away, I would have. It's too late for me."

Declan hangs his head. "I was afraid of that." He rubs his forehead. "I'll keep your secret for her sake. But I'm telling you right now, man; don't put my sister in more danger than she already is."

I swallow hard, hoping I can give Declan a promise that rings true. "I'm here because I want to keep her safe."

Declan lays back down. "I'm going back to sleep. I worked a double two days ago and a full shift yesterday. They keep switching my hours around. I'm constantly dragging."

"That sounds rough. Go back to sleep. I've got her."

"You can go home if you need to, Rome. I'll watch her."

I love the weight of her in my arms. "No. I am not leaving until she is awake and herself again. If I was incapacitated, I wouldn't want to rest unguarded."

Declan closes his eyes. "This is going to be a disaster."

I don't argue because I know he isn't exaggerating.

If I could leave Colette, I would have done so weeks ago. But as it is, I couldn't bear it if she was hurt and I wasn't there to make it all okay. She needs precious little, but right now my own need cannot be quenched. Being the man who gets to hold her while she rests is a desire I have long since wanted to satiate.

I watch over my girlfriend and now her brother while the two of them sleep, hopefully dreaming of better days to come.

22

LET THEM BURN
ROME

Colette's small shifts wake me easily. I'm not sure what time it was that I nodded off to sleep, but the crick in my neck when I right my head from its position of lolling on the back of the couch tells me I've dozed off long enough. Her lashes flutter, and when she finally opens them, it takes half a minute for her eyes to focus.

"Rome?" Her voice is scratchy, so my fingers itch to fetch her a glass of water. But the more pressing need is to hold her, to assure her she was safe while she was unconscious, because I watched over her.

"I'm here," I promise. It's not even close to the dramatic oaths I want to swear to her, but being that she is barely awake and we've been dating only a few months, I rein myself in as much as I am able.

Her mouth falls open as she stares up at me in wonder. "You're in my house. Am I dreaming?"

Her words aren't slurred exactly, but there's a languid rhythm to her cadence that tells me she will need to take it slow today.

"Am I good dream?" It's a question with a sliver of vulnerability laced into the seams. I want to be good for her, which is a slightly higher bar than being good *to* her.

"Beautiful," she marvels at me.

Suddenly I am aware of the bags under my eyes that I have long since made my peace with.

If she notices them, she doesn't say it. "You're a beautiful dream," she coos.

Declan is still sleeping in the middle of the living room floor. I know he doesn't trust me with her, and that's okay. We are new to him. The fact that he didn't actually shoot me bodes well, painting a picture of future days where we can all get along.

I don't get my hopes up that Fintan will ever let old grudges die. I sometimes wish we were still friends, so I had someone outside of my sphere I could bounce ideas off.

For now, I count myself lucky that a member of Colette's family knows about us, and yet I am still upright. Even better, my little cannoli is in my arms.

As I lift her torso so I can examine her face up close, I am astonished anew at how striking she is. I have been staring at her half the night, but I'm not tired of studying the curves of her heart-shaped face. "Incredible," I whisper, entranced at the sight of her stunning features.

It's more than I expect for her to angle her chin up at me, silently asking for a kiss.

When my lips meet hers, the warmth enchants me, drawing me in past all semblance of reason. I've never cared this much about kissing a woman before, but I am a lovesick teenager whenever I get close enough to smell the scent of her hair. She's all vanilla and flowers. I'm a goner whenever she is near. I can see myself being one of those chumps who hold their woman's purse in the store so she can browse unencumbered.

The smallest things set me off, attaching yet more of my heart's strings to her. The visual of doing something as normal as perusing a store together is my new image of happiness.

We should pick out new sheets together. Ones no man has ever laid on with her before. Ones that are only ours.

Ours.

That word settles into my brain and bleeds into the rest of my being. I want so much for my things to be hers.

A hunger rises up in me at the most inopportune time. I want to ravish her, but with her body not quite her own yet, this is hardly the right moment. Add in her brother sleeping a few feet away, and I have to remind myself that my libido cannot call the shots. She is precious to me, fitting perfectly in my arms while our lips take their sweet time introducing our scandal to the morning.

"You shouldn't be here," she warns me after our kiss. Her head isn't quite limp against my forearm, but I am certain she cannot sit up on her own.

"*You* shouldn't be here," I counter, glancing around her home. "This isn't going to work." I frown at the fireplace. "I can't let this coast, little cannoli."

Her lower lip trembles with emotion. "Please, Rome. I was going to tell you eventually."

I cast her a look of disbelief. "I hope you hear how much of a lie that is."

She scrambles to cover her sin. "I want to have told you. Or I want it not to be real. Please..."

"I can't look the other way on this. It's not how I was built."

Tears form in her eyes. "I know it's not ideal, but I have it under control! I don't want us to end. I'll take my medicine every day. I'm so much better than I used to be. I've worked so hard to be normal. Please don't throw me away yet."

My lips purse as I gage her worry with new light. "Throw you away? What do you think is happening here?"

"You're breaking up with me because I'm too much work, but I'm not! I hardly need any help at all anymore. It was a mistake not to take my pills. A stupid mistake I won't make again!"

I kiss her lips harder than usual. When I pull back, it's only an inch so I can brush my nose across hers. "You misunderstand. I'm not going anywhere. I can't stomach you living in the East End if this is how bad it gets." I close my eyes and dig for the truth. "And really, even if you were perfectly healthy, I am never going to be the kind of boyfriend who will tolerate loving someone I cannot look after. Please, tré-sur. Please let me get you a place in Midtown. Somewhere I can come and see you without breaking the law."

Her mouth pops open and her tears still. "What?"

My eyes squinch tight. "I know I'm too much. I'm over-bearing and sometimes I take it too far. I like to make sure my people are looked after. You're it for me, Coletta." The words want to hold themselves back to preserve my pride, but my heart cannot contain them a second longer. "I love you. I'm *in* love with you, and that's not going to change. If you need me, I don't want legal boundaries to stop me from getting to you."

Knowing she cannot always take care of herself kills me. I know myself well enough to understand that I cannot leave this house unless she comes with me. It's a lot to ask—uprooting her just when she has started to settle in one place.

"Yes," she whispers, just as shocked as I am that this is happening. "I'll move to Midtown if it means we can be together more often. I like the look of you in my home."

Declan swears, sitting up from his spot on the floor. "I can't pretend to be asleep anymore if you two are going to be carrying on like this." He pinches the bridge of his nose. "There's only so much covering up I can do for you guys. This is a bad idea."

I ignore Declan's logic because any suggestion that we shouldn't be blissfully together sounds like utter madness. "You should have told me about your tremors, tré-sur. I cannot help you if I don't know how."

She grimaces and turns her chin down, breaking eye contact but keeping close to me all the same. "Can we pretend you don't know any of it? I want you to think I'm strong and capable. I don't want to move closer to you because I'm weak."

It's a laugh to think she could ever be less than both of those things, but the insecurity veiling her eyes tells me the person she has yet to convince is herself.

I kiss the tip of her nose, and then nuzzle it with mine. I'm such a sap now, but I don't care to be the stoic man I was before I fell so irreparably. "I've wanted to be with you more than once a week a long time ago, but I held back because I didn't want to scare you away. So let's blame it on your condition for my sake. It makes me sound like less of a lunatic. But I don't care anymore. I need you, Coletta. Please."

It's my turn to beg. I'll play the part of her debased lover as long as she likes.

Just when I think my heart cannot get any fuller, my treasure kisses me.

Her lips are full and willing, letting me know that the one thing she wants first thing in the morning is me. It's a heady privilege, and not one I take for granted. I want to be the man she kisses every morning, even if it's far too soon or too risky to be feeling such things. I want to kiss her just like this every day, and fill my senses with everything she is to me.

I want this.

I want us.

It's a bad idea. I know. But it's the only thing in the world that makes sense anymore. Staying away from her isn't a hardship I am willing to endure for the sake of propriety any longer. I love this woman in my arms, and I want to sleep beside her as often as she will allow.

I kiss her over and over as a to-do list begins to form. "I will send someone for your things."

"Wait, already?"

"I cannot look after you here," I remind her. "Vampires aren't allowed in the East End."

The gravity of our situation falls on us anew. I worry reality is going to talk her out of the big leap of leaving her house for me.

It's not a fair trade. This is a nice home, to be sure. It's clear she's put thought into the details and made it her own. All she is getting in return is me, along with a clear line in the sand, putting her family and her people on the other side so she can be closer to me.

Declan is a statue, as am I while I wait for Colette to weigh the few meager pros against the mountain of obvious cons.

My chest deflates. I knew I would leap too soon, push too hard, be too much.

When Colette opens her mouth, I am certain my doom is sealed.

"Let's get a place in Midtown that's close to the West End, so you're not too far from work and your family," she rules.

And suddenly, I'm soaring.

"No," Declan butts in. I fight the urge to shove him. "The West End is dangerous. I don't want you moving closer to that area. There are too many dealers there still. Too much halluci-blend. Until the West End is cleaned up, it's a bad idea. If you're really set on this terrible plan, you two should get a place in Midtown closer to the East End."

I'm so grateful, I could kiss the man. "That's fine. I'll take care of it today." I want to reach for my phone, but there are more important things that need tending to, like holding my girlfriend until she can sit up on her own.

I kiss Coletta's soft lips, wondering if there has ever been a man luckier than me.

Declan stands and watches from across the room,

dread painting his features because what we are about to do has never been done.

I will protect her, even if the world and all it holds dear has to burn around us.

Let them burn. We will be safe inside her new home, where I will be with the woman I love.

Love the book?
Leave a review!

23

THE DIVIDED CITY

Enjoy a free preview of "The Divided City", book three in
the Last Deadblood Series.

Two Tangled Hearts
Colette

*L*iving in Mayfield is a constant exercise in hurtling
across new challenges while keeping your head
aimed at your goal. While sometimes my goal is
as pitiful as trying to make it through the day without my
body betraying me and devolving into uncontrollable

spasms, other times there are far more harrowing tasks added to my plate.

And one of those harrowing things is unpacking a box of my sweaters on the other side of my new house. It's been a long day of moving my things from my home in the East End, where my boyfriend could not cross territory lines to visit me, to a new place in Midtown down a dead-end street, where I have the only house on the road.

Even though Rome can go anywhere in Midtown, it would be the scandal of the century if it was found that a vampire and a human were dating.

So we keep our relationship quiet and the witnesses few.

How I wish I could shout our love from the rooftops.

Rome Valentino is the noblest, handsomest and bravest man I have ever known, and for some reason I still can't put my finger on, he has chosen me to read poetry to over the phone every night.

He is also a vampire, and I am a Deadblood. The Last Deadblood, in fact. My blood is the one weapon that can kill a vampire on the spot. Though I would never attack a vampire on my own, my blood has been stolen on many occasions throughout my twenty-five years to create weapons that might murder an entire race of people.

A people I love.

Aside from that obvious hiccup, the fact that I am a

human and Rome Valentino is a vampire makes us an anomaly that people have never seen before.

And hopefully they never will. Keeping our relationship secret is the only way to keep it at all, in my opinion.

Plus, Rome isn't just a vampire, he is *the* vampire—the head of the Valentino family, who owns most of the property in the West End. He comes from old money and isn't afraid to negotiate with the powers that be (and often shouldn't be).

The fact that we are dating is something neither of our families would approve of, not to mention the rest of our respective people.

Despite the creeping worry about what would happen if my father found out about us, there is no part of me that is willing to push our relationship aside. I am hopelessly and madly in love with Rome, even if we are a clear danger to each other.

As I set down the box marked "living room crap" on the floor (thanks, Declan), the trepidation of the unknown zips through my veins. This house is new and unfamiliar, though I know that's no reason to draw a firm opinion. I want to like it here. Rome couldn't visit me in my old house, but here we have a chance at a normal relationship without so much red tape.

It's a nice house, to be sure. The walls have been freshly painted with sky blue in the living room, dandelion yellow in the kitchen, and of course lilac in the two bedrooms. The wooden doorframes, baseboards and wainscoting are bright white, framing the whole one-story home with a lightness that lifts my spirits, even as my back aches from moving about a million and a half boxes. The whole place looks like a feminine haven, and I love it.

Selecting the right home was an exercise in teamwork. I'd picked a two-story house closer to the West End. I wanted a two-story home because then I can challenge myself and prove that I don't need to live with someone. However, Rome and Declan both pointed out that being able to get to my bedroom on a bad day when my tremors call the shots is a blessing worth the cost of sacrificing the self-flagellating stairs.

Darn their solid logic.

When I moved back to my hometown after a decade spent living overseas, I did not anticipate packing back up and hauling my things fifteen miles west just to reopen them in Midtown.

Even though there is nothing odd about a human moving to Midtown, I still feel exposed. Our house is the only abode on this dirt road. I know Rome chose it for its privacy. It's a good thing. A smart move. However, I have no neighbors now, and the dirt road outside is devoid of any traffic.

We have to keep our relationship private. So far only my brother Declan knows and Rome's cousin, Orlando. I'm sure if either of them could shake us out of our syrupy affection for each other, they would.

If I could kick my infatuation with Rome, I would, but he is it for me.

I trot out to my car and take another box from the trunk, carrying it inside toward the bedroom, where Rome is unpacking my things. This box is lighter than the last one, thank goodness.

Even though this house doesn't feel like my home yet, I like seeing Rome in it.

Even as he hangs up my sweaters, I am enamored of his calculating movements. He has far more important things to do today than help me unpack. He even offered to send his men to do the job, but before I could answer, he'd shaken his head. "No. I don't want them in your space. I'll do it."

He hasn't tired, even though I have a great number of unnecessary items.

I pared down as much as I could.

"You're doing it again," he comments without turning his head toward me.

"What am I doing, exactly?"

"You're staring at me. Am I blowing your mind with the way I'm hanging your sweaters? What is it that has you so fascinated, tré-sur?" Then, just to make me laugh, he does a sultry sway, shaking his delicious backside as he shimmies down the closet door like a stripper who dances solely for me.

I love that only I get to see this side of him. The silly, sexy side of Rome is my joy. He's always serious and stoic with everyone else. I get to see his lips curving upwards and the laughter lightening his ice blue eyes. It's like his happiness is a present meant only for me to unwrap.

I move over to him when he rights himself, gluing my front to his spine so I can smooth my palm down his side and over his hip. I kiss the back of his shoulder and bury my face in his white undershirt. My free arm snakes around his taut abdomen. "Yes. It's the way you hang my sweaters. It's making you look absolutely irresistible."

"Remind me to tempt you with home organization more often. Mm." I love when he makes that contented, dreamy sound. Every time it vibrates past his closed lips, my heart swells.

I do that to him. *I* give him those moments of satisfaction.

I kiss the back of his shoulder once more. "I'm glad you're here, helping me with all of this."

"Are you kidding? You're the one who upended your life to move here. Unpacking is the least I can do. Plus, I want to know where everything is. If you're cold, I can't exactly go grab you a sweater if I don't know where they are."

It's the thoughtfulness that makes him so sexy, even

more so than the nuances of his smile. Above his chiseled jaw, his thick black hair, leonine build and stunning features, it's his attention to detail that solidifies his place in my heart, and in my arms.

My hips are curvy while his waist is tapered. I love the distinctions that make our bodies move so beautifully together. He towers over my quaint five feet, yet somehow, we fit perfectly.

"I like the look of you in my home."

"Then I might not leave." It's the second hint he has given me that he would like to be a more permanent fixture here.

I don't know. I don't want him to see me unable to screw off the cap of my meds. I don't want him to know that I sometimes have to take hot baths just to get my muscles to relax themselves. I know the whole point of me moving here was so he could help me if I needed it, but I don't want to need it. I really don't want that to be the reason we live together someday.

Footsteps coming down the hall remind me that we are not alone. Declan and Orlando have been helping us throughout the day. Declan's been moving the boxes while Orlando has busied himself installing the security system. "I just finished reinforcing the entrances," Orlando informs us as he enters the room. "Four keys—one for each of us."

My hands fall away from Rome, though not before I

press another kiss to his body, this time in the center of his spine. I love when he shivers for me. He's so strong and steadfast. To undo his erect posture with a mere kiss?

I have never felt more powerful.

I cast Orlando a bright smile. "Thank you. You're my big sweetie pie. Did you know that?"

Orlando rolls his eyes at the doting only I can get away with. "I think I've heard you say that a few times. In public. Just to embarrass me."

"I say it because it's true." I lean up to press a kiss to his cheek—another thing only I get to do. Orlando has to lean down to accommodate my lack of height. He could keep his posture erect, but deep down, I know he likes the sweetness I bring to his life, or he wouldn't bend to it so often.

Orlando holds out his hand, showing me a small bag no larger than the size of my fist. "This is for you. Do you have a necklace it can go on?"

Rome rolls his eyes, exasperated that Orlando is flubbing up what is apparently supposed to be a precious moment. "You could have put it in a jewelry box. Made it more of a moment."

Orlando's upper lip curls in time with his eyebrow raising. "A moment for what? It's a necessity, not a romantic gift. You should be the one giving it to her."

Rome glowers at his beefier cousin. They look so alike,

but for Orlando's bulkier build. "She won't take it if it's from me."

My head whips from one man to the other. "What are we talking about, here? What's in the bag?"

Orlando opens it for me and dumps the contents into my hand with no finesse.

Gotta love him.

My mouth pops open as I examine the small white gold charm. It's perfectly circular and about the diameter of a coin, though it's nearly half an inch thick. Engraved on the back are two hearts entangled in a way that makes them look incapable of pulling apart. There's a vertical line where the gold splits, running through the circle shape from top to bottom, but it doesn't separate the hearts.

"Wear it," Orlando commands, sounding like a caveman.

"Huh? You got me a charm? Thanks, Orlando."

My big sweetie pie rolls his eyes at me. "Obviously I didn't pick out something so... Rome got it but made me give it to you because apparently we're in middle school."

Rome shoves his cousin toward the door. "Well done. Out you go."

I tilt my head up at Rome, trying to keep up with their odd way of presenting a nice gesture. "Why didn't you want me to know this was from you?"

"Because you would forgive Orlando for being over-bearing. It means something different if a boyfriend asks you to wear a tracker, rather than a head of security."

My shoulders lower. "Oh. This tells you were I'm at?"

"More than that. If you're abducted again, you just do this," Rome takes the charm from my palm and turns it sharply in half where the gold is split down the middle. Just like that, the two hearts are separated, the first on one side, and the second upside-down on the other side. Then he tugs out a chain from beneath his shirt. "I've got one, too. If you do that, mine will vibrate, so I'll know you're in trouble. It's synced to an app on my phone, so I can find you wherever you're at and come get you. If you're having a moment where you can't get to your meds, do the same thing, and I'll come to you and help."

My mouth sets in a firm line. I don't like this, but I can't say that. I know I cannot voice my frustration, because it's not technically with him. I am on edge about needing help from anybody. I can handle myself. I got this far without family and friends.

Then again, I lived with my full-time nurse before I moved back to Mayfield.

Rome seems to hear the current of disgruntlement that I will not voice. "Mine works the same way. If I am taken or if I need you, I do the same to mine, and yours will vibrate."

He rights the circle, so the hearts are together again, and sets it in my palm. Then he takes his own charm dangling from a white gold chain and twists it, setting off a noticeable vibration I can easily detect. Once he rights his, the vibration stops.

He closes my fingers around my charm, his chin lowered in submission because he knows this whole arrangement upsets me. "I need someone to have my back. I want you to know where I'm at in case one of the raids goes south, and I can't get out. How are you with a firearm?"

It takes me a second for his logic to sink in. This is for his protection also, not mine alone.

My lips part as I marvel up at him. He trusts me to get him out of tough situations. I'm his backup.

I swallow hard, this time enjoying the feel of his cool skin surrounding my fist while I hold onto the new piece of jewelry. "I'm the sheriff's daughter. I have four guns in various safes that I'll stash around the house once every-thing is settled."

"One in the salon?"

I scoff. "More than one."

"That's my girl." Rome pulls me into his arms, exhaling deeply when I allow my head to rest against his shoulder. His fingers feather through my brunette waves. "I'm going to sleep much better, now that I know you can watch out for me."

This flip of me looking out for him is not one that I

expected. My chest puffs with pride that he trusts me with something as valuable as his safety.

My mind starts running down this new path, making plans along the way. "I need you to get me dried blood pellets. A few packs. I can't get them myself, but I should have them on hand in case I find you depleted."

I would just feed him my blood, but my blood is deadly to all vampires, so I wouldn't be much help to him in that situation.

Rome squeezes me tighter. "I'll arrange it." I can feel the protective angst in his embrace. "I hate that I can't offer you a safer life. I'm working on it. I'm doing all I can to clean up the West End. It's taking a lot longer than I antici-pated. It's like every time we shut down a halluci-den, another pops up in its place." He kisses the top of my head. "I will make this city safe for you."

That's where my heart sinks. "See, that's the thing. My blood will always be this way. I won't ever be able to live without bulletproof glass and the looming threat of being abducted." I look up into his eyes, vulnerability shining through. "That's something you should know before this gets any more serious."

The corner of Rome's mouth lifts, fixing me with a wry half-smile that suggests I've said something amusing. "Do you think you can scare me away? I'm in this, Coletta."

The note of permanence shines in his beautiful blue

eyes, reminding me that what we have cannot be easily blown away just because the world won't behave.

When his lips caress mine, all worry begins to leave my brain. His arm curls around my hips, coaxing my stomach to his. Oh, how I love the taste of Rome's cinnamon lips. His affection is silky and smooth, passionate and tender.

His hand sneaks down so he can trill his fingers up my thigh, stealing the moment for just the two of us while we have it. His touch climbs under my skirt while his tongue teases mine.

I love that I get this part of him to cherish and hold tightly in my heart.

And now I can protect the best parts of him, so he can come safely home to me.

Read "The Divided City" today!

ABOUT THE AUTHOR

USA Today bestselling author Mary E. Twomey lives in Michigan with her three adorable children. She enjoys reading, writing, vegetarian cooking, and telling her children fantastic stories about wombats.

While she loves writing fantasy, dystopian, and paranormal tales for her readers, Mary also writes romance under the name Tuesday Embers, and cozy mysteries under the name Molly Maple.

Visit her online at www.maryetwomey.com, and sign up for her newsletter, so you never miss a new release.